OTHER
Harlequin Romances
by JOYCE DINGWELL

Clove Orange

by

JOYCE DINGWELL

Harlequin Books

TORONTO • LONDON • NEW YORK • AMSTERDAM
SYDNEY • HAMBURG • PARIS

Original hardcover edition published in 1967
by Mills & Boon Limited

ISBN 0-373-01541-0

Harlequin edition published November 1971

Second printing September 1978

Printed in U.S.A.

CHAPTER ONE

LIBBY. Running up the steps of the B.W.C. with her head high and her heart singing. Just as Mr. Perkins had said.

"At times you'll feel so hopeless," Chief Perkins had warned, "you'll feel like throwing in the sponge. But at times . . . not often . . . it'll be a world full of song."

Today it had been song.

It had been because of Harriet. The last person Libby had expected to find settled had been Harriet Giles. Yet when she had knocked on Mrs. Dawlish's door, Harriet, not her proposed foster-mother, had answered it. "If you've come to fetch me back," adolescent Harriet had greeted, "I'm not coming. Not ever. She says so, too. She says she's asking for me for always." Harriet's black eyes had snapped unmistakably, "So there !"

Curious to think such a truculent announcement could have brought Libby her singing heart, yet not so curious when you remembered that on the previous Harriet trials . . . over six of them . . . Harriet had been waiting at the door to be removed and the abdicating foster-mother been waiting, grimly, for the removal.

Because of this Libby had ignored the truculence and merely reproved mildly, "Not she, darling," while she raised inquiring . . . and hopeful . . . brows to Mrs. Dawlish, hovering quietly in the background.

"Yet," Mrs. Dawlish had concurred sincerely.

So at last Harriet was settled, difficult, tindery, touch-me-not, fourteen-year-old Harriet, and the B.W.C. (officially registered in the State of New South Wales as a charity bearing the name of Because We Care) which dealt in "placing" neglected, or deserted, or orphaned, or apprehended minors, with a view to adjustment, in favourable cases adoption, B.W.C. that took a beating so often and so heartbreakingly, at last claimed a win. It had been, indeed, as Daddy Perkins had said, a world full of song.

Now, as she walked up the sweeping steps, but feeling air, not stairs, beneath her, Libby joyously counted with each rise other heart-singing victories—Thomas. Valerie. David. Miranda.

From a corner of her eye she glimpsed a dark blue station waggon in the street beneath her, and for a moment the song faltered. Yet dark blue station waggons, especially Holden waggons, were everywhere in Sydney. Just because this one was parked in front of the B.W.C. it needn't mean it was *him*.

All the same a lot of the lightness left her. The next rise instead of recalling victories she remembered a failure—Paul.

Had it been because he had the same name as her dead brother that she had persisted so long with Paul? Even Pam, her fellow Because We Care cadet, had remarked on her obstinacy when time after time she had tried again with the boy.

Mr. Perkins, the B.W.C. Chief, the most reasonable and tolerant of men when it came to minors, had even taken her to task over it.

"You're making a fool of yourself over Sellers, Libby, take my advice and give him up."

"That's not in accordance with the B.W.C. principle."

"The B.W.C. gives a hand, but it doesn't keep on giving it. Not to an ill-mannered miscreant such as he has proved himself. What is it about this lad? You've always shown judgment before."

But there was never Paul before, Libby could have cried out. The same age . . . if *my* Paul had not died. The same flick of hair over the brow, the same brown eyes. If she had been honest she would have admitted many differences. Her brother Paul's steady, not shifting, glance, his firm, not lax, mouth. Character, not just nothing there at all.

But Libby had not been honest. Her hungry heart, still crying out for a boy who had died too young, whose loss had been all the worse because the sister and brother had been orphaned less than a year, had known no reason.

"Please, Mr. Perkins, try again with Paul Sellers," she begged.

"It's a risk. He's not only dishonest, he's—well, un-savoury, too. He could ruin the B.W.C. You know how ready people are to throw stones."

"Another go, please, Daddy Perkins." Libby had blue eyes, and two top front teeth that fastened engagingly on her full lower lip when she was in stress. Old Mr. Perkins, anyway, found them engaging.

"Oh, very well," he had weakened.

An hour later the Chief had told Libby that Paul was going up to Clove Orange, Mr. Pierce Hardway's large herbary on the westered slopes of the New South Wales Blue Mountains. "Mr. Hardway has been a rock to build on to B.W.C.," Mr. Perkins said, as he had said many times before of this Pierce Hardway. "Besides donating substantially he has regularly accepted our boys."

Libby knew she should have been grateful on behalf of Paul, but the bleak realization that he was going out of Sydney, not stopping, as she had hoped, had made her unreasonable. She had commented unfairly on Pierce Hardway's acceptance of the B.W.C. boys : "Cheap herb harvesters" and at once been reproved by the Chief.

"Libby!"

She had had the grace ... or the wisdom ... to climb down.

"I didn't mean that, of course. I—I'm just sorry it has to be so far away for Paul."

"A mere seventy or so miles! Only several hours! Is this an Australian talking?" It wasn't, it was a New

Zealander, but before Libby could inform him of that, could wriggle out of the situation in which she had placed herself, Mr. Perkins had said with an unmistakable significance, "Sellers is extremely fortunate to land a place like Clove Orange. I only hope you'll point that out to him."

"I shall." Libby had been prudently contrite. After all, seventy miles was better than sending Paul back to the detention home, which, by that note in Mr. Perkins' voice, had been the only alternative.

She had packed Paul's things, fussed over him in the way she always did with Paul.

"You will try to settle, won't you, Paul."

He had made no response.

"Paul, dear!"

"Oh, stow it, Miss Meadows."

"But, Paul—"

"I'm going. That's enough, isn't it?"

"It's not enough. I want you to try."

"Try what?"

"Oh, Paul!" sighed Libby.

"Try this?" Seventeen-year-old Paul had actually made an amatory advance on her, which Libby should have reported at once. But she hadn't. There had been too big an ache in her heart.

"Try," she had repeated, avoiding his arms and escaping weakly out of the door.

She had watched him go down the B.W.C. steps in the company of a tall, lean, hard, brown man.

"That's the famous Pierce Hardway of Clove Orange," Pam had said by her side. "He'll be good for that young fiend."

"He looks tough." Libby's senses had rebelled—for Paul—against the toughness.

"He is, but there must be kindness there, too. None of our lads have asked to leave, after all."

"Paul needs sympathy."

"That's the last thing he does need. Libby, what's got into you with that boy?"

Whatever it was, it still had been there when Pierce Hardway, the tall, lean, hard, brown herb-grower of Clove Orange, had returned Paul to the B.W.C. within the month.

Libby had been in the office when the two, the man, the youth, had come in.

"Back again?" Mr. Perkins had sounded unsurprised at the event.

Pierce Hardway had lit a pipe and taken his time in doing it. Unwillingly it had come to Libby that here was a man who would always take time, especially with a boy. He would not be impulsive, unreasonable, unfair. But she had not wanted to think like that, not of someone who had brought Paul back again, much as she wanted Paul. It made a failure of both him and her. Foolishly, she had stepped forward and asked the boy, "Are you all right?"

For the first time since he had entered the room the herb man had seemed to be aware of Libby.

He had turned in his characteristic slow, easy way and looked at her. But the flame in the grey eyes had been quick, not slow. It had been quite angry.

"No, he is severely beaten. If you look, you will find the bruises. He has been starved, deprived, victimized, maltreated."

"Don't be ridiculous!" Libby had snapped indignantly.

"Don't *you* be ridiculous, stepping out like that and bleating 'Are you all right?' The boy has had the same treatment as the others, which I pride myself is good treatment."

"Love?" Libby had barely whispered. Young ones must have love.

"He has no taste for it."

The man must have decided she was to immature, or

too ignorant, to argue with, for he had turned back to Mr. Perkins.

"I'm sorry, sir," Libby heard him say. "There was a matter of a theft . . . there was something else." He half-glanced towards Libby.

"I understand," Mr. Perkins construed. To Libby he directed, "Wait outside with Sellers."

In the corridor Libby appealed, "You didn't, did you, Paul? Steal? Misbehave?"

"He was a slave-driver. He wanted cheap labour for his blasted weeds. Look, Libbo, I could tell you a few things—"

"Miss Meadows." She had said it weakly as usual—but there had been no weakness in her for the herb man. As he had gone down the B.W.C. steps to the street again she had called after him over the balustrade.

"I would advise you in future to pay for your staff, not try to get things done on the cheap." Her young voice had rung cool and clear.

He had turned in that easy, deliberate way of his and looked up at her.

After a long moment, instead of the biting rage she had expected . . . and deserved? . . . he had drawled, "I'm sorry for you, young woman, you look the proud sort, and it's always the hardest of all for the proud sort to take things back."

"I'll be taking nothing back," she retorted.

"Oh, yes, you will, because you're honest as well as proud. I've had experience with people like you, and I know how hard—but necessary—honesty is."

"You're wrong." She had said it forcefully but a little uncertainly, hating the uncertainty but still keenly conscious of it.

"I give you"—he had estimated a deliberate moment—"a month." He had turned again and gone.

He had been three days out.

Mr. Perkins, always weak when it came to Libby, had

tried once again with Paul, and this time even Paul's personal sponsor had been shocked and disillusioned.

"Paul, did you—did you—"

"Of course I did, and I will again. Look, Libbo, I'm sick of your Sunday school bleating. You're not a bad sort when you're not mooning around and saying 'Paul, did you?' I could even—" The bold eyes, all at once *not* like her brother's, narrowed slyly and significantly.

In that instant the scales had fallen from Libby's own eyes.

"You're cheap," she said, suddenly sickened.

"Yes, dear."

"You're not worth worrying about."

"Then why are you worrying?" There had been confidence bred of long indulgences in the young voice.

"I'm not worrying any more." Libby had turned on her heel and gone out. Paul had been sent to a farm school. The matter had ended.

Though it hadn't *really* ended, of course. Being the honest person he had said she was she had had to face the herb man and admit she had been wrong.

She had done it, stiffly but fully, unwillingly, but keeping nothing back.

"Thank you," he had said drily when she had done, then he had reached for his pipe.

"That," he had drawled, "is the hardest thing you've ever worked at, I'd warrant. Making allowances for that difficulty, I will overlook the unmistakable lack of warmth."

"Is one ever warm over an apology?"

"One shows more humility and less challenge. You challenged me in every syllable. You've been found wrong and yet you fight even while you admit defeat. Which makes it no win for me."

"Do you have to win?"

His grey eyes had found and held hers.

"I don't make a point of it unless I happen to be interested." He had waited for her to question him, and, indeed, she had wanted to flash, "What is it that interests you, then?"

But she had closed her lips, left the apology at that and left him.

Several times entering or leaving B.W.C. she had seen him in the distance. She had heard Mr. Perkins laud him, Pam tell how the Hilliard boy had thrived, Rob Benson settled in.

But like that "challenge in every syllable" of his, the smoulder had remained in her. The instinct to fight even in defeat had persisted—when it came to this man.

She had avoided him. It was not just the shame of having been wrong and having had to admit it, it was also the knowledge that he was aware that the smoulder was still in her, the fight. Most of all she had the disturbing impression that Pierce Hardway sensed there was a reason for it all, and intended to know it, even, perhaps, intended to meet her half way in it . . . hadn't he the reputation with B.W.C. of being a most exceptional man? . . . and Libby, still too raw, too newly bereft, shrank from intrusion, even kindly intrusion. Anyway, could that tall, lean, hard brown man ever be *really* kind?

"I'm spoiling my moment of singing," Libby said to herself now, mounting the top step with a bound. "Today is triumph, not failure. I won't even think of Mr. Clove Orange." She laughed at her name for him.

She was still smiling as she went into the office.

"Harriet's 'fixed'! It's Mrs. Dawlish . . . they took to each other like bread and jam," she announced.

"It's been a good day altogether," beamed Mr. Perkins. "Pam had a fair report on Ronald Lighton. And just now we've placed our little Miss Frith."

"Barbary? Barbary Frith?" exclaimed Libby.

"Yes."

"But that's wonderful news! I mean it will be if she settles down this time."

"She will—with her brother Scott."

"But Scott is—Scott is up at that herbary."

"You mean Clove Orange? Pierce Hardway's?"

"Yes." Libby looked questioningly at Daddy Perkins.

"You're quite right. She's joining him," Mr. Perkins said quite calmly.

Not calmly, Libby objected, "But he doesn't take girls."

"He hasn't taken any previously. Barbary will be his first."

"He has only provision for boys."

"He did have."

"He would need a woman with a girl," she pointed out.

"He has."

"He would need someone else . . . well, for a start, anyway." It was a strict rule of the B.W.C. that a staff member of the same sex always accompanied a ward for a few days if they went out of the city, saw them settled in. Perhaps Pam—

But:

"You will be going, Libby," said Mr. Perkins.

"Daddy" Perkins, though the most reasonable and tolerant of men as well with the minors as with those who attended the minors, none the less was Chief, and as such commanded compliance.

"Yes, Mr. Perkins," Libby said compliantly. She inquired, "When?" and was told "Today. Take the Mini."

"Yes, Mr. Perkins," Libby intoned again.

She went out of B.W.C. and got into the Society's Mini to drive to suburban Torrington, the cottage home where Barbary was currently housed.

A dozen why-couldn'ts irked her as she dodged the agile little car between the city traffic. Why couldn't Pam have accompanied Barbary up to Clove Orange? Why couldn't the herb man have taken her back with him, for obviously that dark blue Holden at the foot of the B.W.C. steps had been his.

But she did not fume "Why must Barbary go at all?" for therein lay a tale.

Even though Daddy Perkins had said that Barbary would settle down this time because she would be with her brother, it was more the other way about. Scott would settle. And Scott settling was more important, for he had reached touchy fifteen, he was prone, impressionable, vulnerable, and he had got in with a wrong type.

The two children had been orphaned tragically and suddenly in a road accident, yet not so suddenly that the dying parents had not had time to whisper to their son Scott: "See to Barbary."

He had taken it too literally, he had even stolen for Barbary, and that was where the Child Welfare had stepped in, and at their heels the B.W.C. The Society had pleaded to take over Scott, and, as usual, been given a favourable hearing, for the Welfare thought highly of Because We Care.

Barbary, too, had come to B.W.C., for the distant relative who had taken on the pair wanted no more of either of them after the thieving episode.

Obviously the brother and sister should have been kept together, but one was an orphaned child and the other an apprehended one, so by necessity Barbary had been put in a B.W.C. cottage home and Scott in a B.W.C. corrective one.

Barbary had been transferred several times since. "Not naughty," each housemother had proffered, "but unsettled."

Scott's history had not been so mild—until he had gone to Clove Orange. After that there had been smoother waters—yet evidently not smooth enough, for Barbary now was going to Pierce Hardway's herbary to join Scott.

And I, grumbled Libby, am taking her.

She turned the small B.W.C. car with its "Help us help our children" inscribed in gold lettering, and an address to enable a benefactor to do so, up the Torrington drive. Barbary was waiting on the verandah.

"I'm going up to Scotty," she greeted.

"I know, darling. I've come to take you."

"Today?"

"Yes. It's not far ... only seventy miles ... several hours." Daddy Perkins had said that, Libby remembered, when she had protested for Paul. Odd, but she never thought about Paul now, only about the embarrassment with Pierce Hardway that the wretched business had brought.

"Aunty Hope has packed my bag," said Barbary.

"Yes, darling." How pathetic these children's worldly possessions, Libby knew from experience—a thin case with a gym tunic, bits of underwear and the inevitable collection of old Christmas cards.

"Tied with ribbon," nodded Barbary, and Libby realized she must have been thinking aloud. "Aunty Hope gave it to me. It's pink ribbon. Can we go to Scotty now?"

"After I have a word with Aunty Hope."

Libby went in and collected Barbary's bag, receiving the usual assurance proffered by all Barbary's cottage mothers that Barbary had not been difficult, only unsettled.

"Mr. Hardway told me yesterday over the phone that it's the same with Scott," said Hope Brent, "a restlessness and an unease, something vastly to be preferred to rebellion, he admits, which has been the pattern in all the other places Scott has been sent to, but still leaving room for improvement. Hence," smiled Aunty Hope Brent, "Clove Orange."

As Libby did not comment, she sighed admiringly, "What a man!"

"The herb baron?"

"Who, Libby?" queried Aunty Hope.

"Mr. Clove Orange. Oh, don't look so put out, Hope, I mean Mr. Hardway, of course."

"I am put out when you speak like that of a person like him. He's a—"

"Rock to build on," nodded Libby impatiently. "I've heard that song before."

"Well, he is. Now a bachelor like Pierce Hardway—"

"Is he?"

"A bachelor? Of course. That's why he has never included girls among his wards before. Barbary is only being accepted because of Scott."

"He has a woman there now," said Libby flatly, "and I didn't mean is he a bachelor, I meant is that fantastic handle really his name."

"Do you doubt it?" asked Hope Brent rather sniffily.

"Yes, I think he was christened Perce." Libby's voice was pert. "As for Clove Orange, it's absurd."

"Really, Libby, what's got into you? Generally it's the children you think of, not yourself."

"I wasn't thinking of myself . . . at least—"

"You were thinking of your red face over the Paul Sellers affair. Oh, yes, we all heard about that."

Libby was silent a while, then decided to agree. It was the easiest—and least painful. She could not say, "No, Hope, it wasn't so much the Sellers affair as my reason behind it all . . . the reason of my dead brother, of my dead parents, of people treading where, just now, I can't bear anyone even to lay a gentle finger."

"I suppose you're right," she admitted aloud. "Is this the bag?"

"Yes. God bless her." Hope kissed Barbary who had come impatiently in to see what was holding things up, and said, as Barbary would expect, "Do as you're told, dear."

Once out of the tangle of traffic and on the slightly less congested Western road, Barbary asked, "Why do grown-ups say do as you're told? I might be told to shoot Warren's water pistol at that traffic policeman, I might—"

"Barbary, have you Warren's water pistol?"

"No, he took it back, mean sneak. Why do grown-ups—"

"Grown-ups wouldn't say shoot your water pistol, Barbary." A believer in diversion, Libby diverted, "Look how small that plane is getting." She pointed to the west-ered sky and a westbound craft.

"What happens to the people in it when it gets smaller, too?"

"No, darling, it's the distance."

"What's distance?"

"Miles between things. Like it was with you and Scott. Now there won't be distance any longer. You'll be to-gether at Clove Orange."

"What's Clove Orange?"

"Mr. Hardway's herbary where you're going."

"But what is it?"

By the time Libby had told her they were leaving Penrith behind them and climbing the foothills of the Great Dividing Range.

Today the Blue Mountains really were blue. Postcard blue. Artist's blue. No right to exist in fact at all.

"It's the wind," Libby said a little absently. At Bar-bary's round-eyed glance she explained about the wind releasing the oil in the eucalyptus trees so that the leaves gleamed bluely and painted the mountains that colour.

"If I took a fistful of air would it be blue?" asked Barbary.

"No, it just *seems*, like the aeroplane *seemed* small."

"I like real things, not seem things," said Barbary plaintively.

"Then we'll have a real thing, darling, an ice as soon as we reach Katoomba."

As they sat in the cool soda cavern in the popular mountain resort with a pink pinnacle before them com-plete with chocolate sauce, marshmallow, nuts, and all the other usual trimmings, Libby wondered a little dub-iously if she had done the right thing. A herbary sug-gested herby sort of foods, not pink pinnacles with chocolate sauce, marshmallow, nuts, and if Barbary turned down the thyme omelette, or the saffron stew, which presumably Clove Orange might serve, he, the herb baron, might decide to demand why.

"Beaut," awarded Barbary with a last lick round of her spoon, and Libby remembered the thin case in the car with only the tunic, the underwear, the bundle of old Christmas cards tied with pink ribbon and nothing else, and decided she didn't care a hoot, herb baron and all.

They came out into the crisp, cool mountain air and continued west. Libby showed Barbary the Marked Tree where the explorers Blaxland, Wentworth and Lawson had blazed a trail across the Blue Mountains, and she noted uneasily at the same time that Barbary had a certain marked expression herself. Having dealt with juniors all her several working years, she recognized that expression at once. Queasy tum. It must be the chocolate sauce, marshmallow, and nuts.

"Are you all right, Barbary?" she asked.

"Yes. Any more curves?"

On the mountains it was all curves, but Libby took them as gently as she could. Afterwards she thought she should have spun round them, brought the climax earlier, got it over *before* Clove Orange.

For, having descended from Mount Victoria into the sleepy loveliness of the Hartley Valley, having skimmed along an offshoot ribbon of road for four more miles, having turned off at a swinging sign indicating Clove Orange to run along a thickly wooded way for several more miles, Libby, suddenly inhaling airs she had never inhaled before, turned excitedly to the little girl to say, "Isn't it the very breath of heaven?" to see that Barbary was unmistakably not up to breaths, even heavenly ones.

"Are you all right, Barbary?" she asked anxiously.

"Y-yes."

She was ... but she was not five minutes after. By

such time the B.W.C. car had pulled up at the herbary, a large one-storeyed house looking rather like the huge hub of a wheel, for it was completely surrounded by airy dormitory wings, and the herb baron, Mr. Clove Orange, Pierce Hardway himself, had come down the sweeping front steps to take the little girl's bag.

But before he removed the bag from the car, he removed Barbary . . . and it happened. Chocolate sauce, marshmallow, nuts, the lot.

"I'm sick," wept Barbary loudly.

Libby could have wept, too, when she looked at Pierce Hardway's once immaculate shirt. She dared not look at his face.

Always situations of this sort had propelled Libby into immediate and efficient action. Just as some people type as though the keys are an extension of their fingertips, instinctively Libby had sprung forward to relieve and allay almost as though she herself was a child extension.

But today she stood helpless and befuddled, her arms that should have supported Barbary in her spasms hanging stupidly slack. All she was aware of was horror, horror that anyone could *dare* be sick not only before but over this man.

Then even as she stood staring frozenly at the tall, lean, hard brown figure she made an astonishing discovery. He was tall, lean, brown, but not hard. Not, anyway, to Barbary. Why, he was tender. Tender? The herb baron?

He did the right things in the right sequence. First the soothing, the assurance that all was well, and then, Libby still standing like a mummy, he bore the child into the house, obviously in the direction of a bathroom. By the time Libby had scrambled after them he had Barbary's frock unbuttoned and the basin filled with warm water.

"Stand still, my sweetheart," he was intoning soothingly. "What a little glutton it is, it ate so much it brim-

med over. If you don't watch you'll be like that man
from Antigua."

Barbary hiccoughed, cried some more, then asked,
"What man?"

"Well, as I said he came from Antigua, and his wife
said to him, 'What a pig you are,' because, you see,
Barbary, by gobbling so much, he had lost his figua."
To Libby he tossed, "A clean towel, please."

He was wonderful. Libby just couldn't credit it. This
couldn't be the same man who had returned Paul to
B.W.C., returned him definitely, standing no nonsense,
Paul, tough, rebellious, callous, quite as large Paul,
silenced, for once, as he stood by this man's side, only
speaking up for himself *out of earshot* of Pierce Hardway.

"There you are, Princess, sweet as an apple again," the
voice was intoning. "All fit for Scott."

"Are you going to tell Scotty?" asked Barbary tear-
fully.

"That his sister's a good girl, not a squeak out of
her even when I scrubbed pretty hard?"

"That I was sick," gulped Barbary, "all over—" She
finished in spasms of laughter, for Pierce Hardway, evidently practised in the vulnerable spots of the young,
had her doubled up with the tickles. By the time she had
recovered he had left her to Libby and apparently gone
out also to clean up.

He was back almost at once; there was not even an
opportunity for Barbary to discuss him with Libby, as
undoubtedly from the look of the bright eyes and moistened lips Barbary ardently intended. Little girls, Libby
knew, were quick to worship.

"Scott is due from the basil planting in"—he glanced
at his watch—"exactly three minutes." Her second
glance was at Libby. "The working hours here are
strictly recorded"... a deliberate pause ... "my staff are
paid."

He was leading the way through the house to the

verandah. Libby had a quick impression of many large airy rooms, but it was only a hazy picture, for she was thinking guiltily of leaning over the B.W.C. balustrade to call after the tall, lean man striding now in front of her, "I advise you in future to pay for your staff." But perhaps he had only attended to this *after* that advice of hers, perhaps—

"I had," drawled Pierce Hardway, opening the screen door, "always paid." His look at Libby was barely that, more the merest flick.

"Scott!" shrieked Barbary as a crowd of boys advanced to the house. "Scotty!" and she ran down the steps, a much cleaner version than she had been carried up.

Once Scott had satisfied himself she was sound in limb, he discarded her as all fifteen-year-old brothers discard small sisters half their age.

"He'll be all right now," approved Pierce Hardway with satisfaction. "He needed that assurance."

"But," interrupted Libby pointedly, "how will Barbary be?" A seven-year-old girl needed her own age group, needed other little females. Though Pierce Hardway, of course, would only look at this situation from his own male angle.

"I've been considering that," the man beside her said blandly. "I've decided to make Barbary a forerunner."

"Forerunner?" echoed Libby.

"Of girls as well as boys."

He would! He just would think of everything. Just as . . . and Libby felt herself retreating as a mollusc retreats at the touch of a finger . . . he would consider, and undoubtedly had considered, *her.* She recalled her strong sense of his readiness to meet her halfway that day. Now she experienced it again. But she didn't want this man's sympathy, anyone's sympathy; she had to get over Paul, her brother Paul, as she had got over her parents. By herself. In only that way could she ever surface, surface completely, again.

"Have the other boys handy sisters?" she asked casually, over-casually.

"Only a few, but that's not the real point. For a home to emerge from a house it must have both male and female." His eyes met hers for a rather long moment.

"A female as young as Barbary?" she rushed in.

"You beggar my point. Sufficient to say just now that Barbary is my beginning, I hope."

"Scott doesn't appear all that enthusiastic," she dared, indicating Scott's indifference.

"Are you blind, or have your few years as a cadet not taught you the natural reactions of a boy of Scott's age?" he said coldly. "Scott is overjoyed. At any moment now he'll tell Barbary to pipe down, even clip her across the ears. This house will become his home."

She was looking at him in estimation. "How did a herb baron become a psychologist?" she inquired.

"Baron?" he questioned.

"Aren't you the owner of the biggest herbary in the state?"

"I have never had time to assess that, but I can assure you I have no blue blood in me, any reason to add a title to my name." His voice was dry.

"*Is* it your name?" she dared.

He looked back at her. "You have a point there. It is not."

"I knew it!" she said triumphantly.

"Good for you," he awarded. "So what is my name?"

"Percy." She smiled thinly at him.

"Wrong. It's Pearce."

"You just said it wasn't Pierce."

"It isn't, not the penetrating, perforating Pierce I mean, it's P-e-a-r-c-e." He spelled it.

"Then—?"

"Someone allotted me Pierce instead. No doubt after they had seen what I had done with this bush."

"What had you done?"

He looked at her incredulously. "Are you serious?"

"Yes. What had you done?"

He opened his mouth, then he closed it. "No," he decided, "I'll show you instead, I'll show you tomorrow."

"I won't be here tomorrow," she pointed out.

"But most certainly you will. Mr. Perkins is undoubtedly expecting you to do the usual thing, stop with the new child until the child is settled in."

"But Barbary has already settled."

"How can you know? Things are different when night falls." At his own words he glanced to the window, and Libby followed the glance. Why, it was almost dark.

"That is another reason," he nodded.

"What do you mean?"

"I mean even if it was not a law of B.W.C. I'd still not permit you to leave here at this time of day."

"How ridiculous! Do you think I'm not used to driving in the dark?"

"I doubt if you are used to driving in the dark *here*. Mists rise. We can almost count on them at this time of year in this particular corner. One is swirling in right now."

She looked at the window again, suspecting him. The great gob of grey vapour that had risen since she had last looked, only a moment before, now appalled her. The silver wisps touched the glass silently, but every now and then the accumulated moisture was released and it trickled down in thin witch fingers. She realized it would be impossible to leave.

"Yes, even for me," he confirmed, reading her thoughts, "and I know every inch of the track."

"You should have warned me," she said crossly; she felt she could not stop here in this house—with him—overnight. "I would have left at once."

"That I readily believe, for you were not overly concerned, were you, for the sick child."

"That's not true!" Libby exclaimed. "You took over before I could step forward myself."

"You took a long time in the advance," he reminded her thinly.

"That was because I was horrified."

"Horrified?"

"To think that Barbary ... to think that she—she—" The words trailed off.

"And why not?" he intervened smoothly, anticipating what she had not said. "Vomiting is a childish occurrence, I should imagine it happens quite frequently during a parenthood."

"But you're not a—"

"Parent? Not yet. But I have the usual hopes." He had taken out his pipe. "In which case I see nothing wrong and much to be desired in practising to be less the ogre than some people have pre-established me." He looked at her squarely.

"I was just embarrassed for both of us, for Barbary and for me," Libby said inadequately.

"For you only," he corrected. "The child didn't come into it. Well"—tapping the pipe—"it was only a bilious attack after all, scarcely worth these heated words."

If they were heated, thought Libby, the heat was certainly not on his side. He stood cool, composed, remote.

"Having agreed you can't leave tonight," he said, "perhaps you would like to see your room."

"Is it ready?" she asked.

"Certainly. I expected you to stop. Don't forget I've had B.W.C. wards before."

"Well, I wish I'd expected it," said Libby. "I brought no clothes."

"I think if you had looked in the car boot you would have found that you had. I rather anticipated this attitude from you, so I had a few words today while in Sydney with Pamela."

"Pam Burnett?"

"Yes. Your fellow cadet."

"How dared you?" snapped Libby.

"Look," he indicated in answer, and she saw that outside the window was nothingness now, just a world of blinding vapours. "Isn't it just as well I had those few words with Pam, otherwise you would have been obliged to borrow from one of the boys, the female complement here being either too small or too large." For her information he explained, "Barbary. My housekeeper, Mrs. Dawson. Then I don't think," he went on with a slight smile, "you would have been happy in denims and plaid shirt, our usual male garb."

Libby was not to be placated. "Even if there was no history of mists," she accused bitterly, "you would still have had that word with Pam."

"Of course. Isn't settling in the ward a routine thing?"

"And don't you demand everything to be cut and dried and routine? Take—take Paul." She had not intended to say that for, Paul, the B.W.C. Paul, meant nothing to her now, had meant nothing for months.

He looked at her a long moment, so long that in the end she turned her own glance away.

"That was something else I expected," he said, "from you."

He had been leading her down a maze of corridors. Now he stopped.

"Here is your room. I'll have one of the boys bring in that bag."

"That Pam packed."

He ignored that. "Dinner is in half an hour."

"Herb stew?" she asked sarcastically.

He ignored that, too.

CHAPTER TWO

THE room, like the rest of the rooms that she had noticed briefly as she passed through them, like the entire house she remembered from pulling up at the centre "hub" and seeing the surrounding dormitory "spokes," was wide, spacious, airy. With its substantial adjoining box-room, the herb baron could even have made a family unit of it. And perhaps that was what he had visualized. Male and female, he had said. A home, to emerge from a house, must have both sexes. She remembered that long, enigmatical glance.

She opened the case that one of the boys had brought in ... Gordon, she had recognized at once, quite a problem to B.W.C., at least he had been, though come to think of it she had not heard any mention of him, or his misdeeds, for months.

"Hullo, Miss Meadows," Gordon had greeted, and he had carefully lifted her bag on to the bed. To say the least she had been surprised. Gordon had been distinctly ill-mannered. Not a really bad boy, but—well, a lout. She had been a little dismayed as he had quietly left the room, gently shutting the door behind him. Not another mark on the credit side, surely, for Mr. Clove Orange!

Opening up the case she had found another reason to be disgruntled. Pamela had forgotten nothing. She had also put in sufficient for several weeks, not several days. Had *he* instructed that as well? And yet why should he instruct it? Obviously he had as little time for her as she had for him. Except that he was cut and dried and routine, as she had flung at him just now, he would not have had her anywhere near his precious herbary. But because the establishing of the wards was the routine procedure, and indubitably he believed strongly in conformity, Mr. Clove Orange had followed the rule. To be quite fair to the man that strict adherence to the B.W.C. law that he had just quoted had had only the children in view and no malice towards her, but did he have to be so definitely B.W.C.-minded when he was not even, as she was, attached to the Charity, when he was only a spectator? And why was he so interested in children, in Because We Care? Why?

There were literally hundreds of charitable societies in New South Wales, scores of them slanted to the young, yet he had chosen this social outlet for his good works, acceptable to the B.W.C. no doubt, but not, and Libby put a dress on a hanger that Pam had also packed, acceptable to her. *She disliked Mr. Clove Orange.*

She carried the frock on its hanger to a large built-in wardrobe. She had no intention of staying after to-morrow, that is, of course, if Barbary was still settled in, though there seemed little doubt about that, but a dress might as well hang as huddle, and she slid open the door.

At once a fragrance accosted her; accost was the only word, for the fresh spiciness just didn't steal on the senses, it claimed them, claimed them poignantly, pungently, yet at the same time almost unbelievably sweetly. She stood breathing in the fragrant air. It was a summer scent, a scent of sunsoaked stone walls, mown hay, the breath of young flowers, yet through the warmth came the sharp reality of cinnamon, orris and cloves. Simply standing letting the aromatic airs steal around her was sheer joy.

She stood so long and so entranced she did not hear the first dinner bell.

Indeed the second bell had gone, and a boy had come to fetch her for the evening meal before Libby emerged from her pleasant dalliance, emerged with a start, for she had been years away, fifteen years in fact; she had been balancing on a chair in her grandma's room to see what she could dress up in when a scent like this one had entangled her heart, a summer smell of sunsoaked walls, hay, the breath of young flowers and the other that a child had not recognized but an adult now did— orris, cinnamon and cloves.

What was it? Where did it come from?

Libby leaned forward now to investigate, but the boy at the other side of the door tapped and called, "It's dinnertime, Miss Meadows. Will you come, please, Mr. Hardway says."

Libby stepped away from the wardrobe and from fifteen years ago, ran a comb quickly through her acorn-brown hair, then opened the door.

"Toby!" she exclaimed.

"Yes, Miss Meadows. Didn't you know I was here?"

"I knew you had been directed to Clove Orange, but I didn't know whether—whether you had stayed," Libby said discreetly. Toby West had been taken over by B.W.C. when a Government orphanage had thrown up its hands and given Toby up. Like Gordon, he was not really bad, but he was a hopeless wanderer. He had gone walkabout from no less than nine homes, which prompted Libby to appeal of Toby now: "How long?"

"I've been here eight weeks and I'll stop eighty years if he'll keep me." Toby was dead serious.

It was redundant to say, "You must like it, Toby," so Libby said nothing, just followed the boy down the passage to the dining-room.

It was such a big room it was not dwarfed by the quite immense table spanned across its entire length. Everyone, Libby could see at once, sat at the table at the same time; no separate meals for adults here. In spite of the number of diners, the boys, Barbary, Pierce Hardway and an elderly woman, presumably Mrs. Dawson, the housekeeper, were seated quite comfortably. But as Libby entered, all, with the exception of the housekeeper who was busy serving up but who looked across to give Libby a welcoming smile, rose. Barbary had to be prompted by Pierce Hardway, who, of course, would have to prompt himself. Or so Libby ungenerously thought. Just a gesture for the boys, she decided contemptuously; ordinarily he would have kept such niceties for more distinct occasions than the routine evening meal, and for more acceptable females than Libby Meadows.

Three of the boys did not sit down again when Libby sat, they lined up by Mrs. Dawson and began passing round the plates. As Libby bowed her head for grace, spoken at a prompting nod by a boy she remembered being returned to B.W.C. several times but now looking as settled in as both Gordon and Toby looked, she caught a whiff from the big brown goulash waiting to be consumed. It was redolent with the usual mouth-watering additions she sniffed at once—but with something else she did not know.

· In that annoying way he had of reading her, Pierce Hardway, on her left, said, "Oh, but you do recognize it, for didn't you anticipate Herb Stew?"

"Is it?" she asked.

"No, it's beef, of course, but there are additions."

At her raised brow he said, "Fennel and coriander."

"I've never heard of them."

"Then you are the only one among us. While you dallied tonight in your room I took Barbary quickly round the herbary."

"But the mists—"

"The mists have gone. They're like that." He shrugged.

"In which case I could be gone, too." Libby was looking towards the window. She saw that the night was clear again, the vapours and wisps completely dispersed.

He ignored that. He said, "Why did you take so long? You haven't changed your dress."

She could not say, "I was fifteen years away, I was standing on a chair and looking in my granny's wardrobe for clothes to dress up in," so she said instead, "You're very perceptive, Mr. Hardway."

"It's necessary with a houseful of young."

She took an appreciative forkful from the plate in front of her. It was quite delicious.

"Why is there a houseful of young, Mr. Hardway?" she asked. Almost she had said Mr. Clove Orange.

"A B.W.C. representative asks that?" His brows were up.

"Oh, I'm sure I'm very pleased, I mean it's what the Society wants, but why have *you* responded so fully?"

"But surely you have informed me of that already." Now the brows were down in one straight line. "It's for cheap labour."

She flushed at that, bowed her head and bit again into the goulash. It was one of the nicest dishes she had ever eaten, and she murmured as much, rather in surprise.

"Why shouldn't it be?" he asked at once.

"No reason," she admitted, "just an unfamiliarity on my part." She wondered how Barbary was taking the new fare, and looked a little apprehensively at the small girl. But Barbary was tucking in with undisguised gusto.

"The young," said Pierce Hardway, following Libby's glance, "don't question, they simply react."

"A reaction like that after what she has been eating is rather surprising," proffered Libby, remembering the ice-cream binge at Katoomba.

"Don't forget she lost most of it," he grinned. Before Libby could murmur another regret for the episode, he went on, "It's amazing, really, just how the kids do take to this fare. When I first started off with the wards I used only familiar herbs like parsley and mint, but in no time beef stew demanded origano, and potato pie cried out for bergamot."

"What is origano and what is bergamot?" asked Libby.

"I'll show you tomorrow." Before she could argue that she would be gone tomorrow he helped her, for by now the goulash was finished, to a sweet of baked apple and thick cream. *And geranium leaves.*

"Apple-scent geranium leaves," he said. "Don't be frightened of them, Miss Meadows."

Gingerly, Libby bit into a leaf. It was crisp—and it was delicious. "I'm astounded," she said.

"I'm not. I would have been, though, had you *not* liked it. Another serving?"

"Goodness, no. Can I help with the dishes?"

"Neither you, nor I, nor Mrs. Dawson helps with those. No, the boys take over ... it's only a matter, really, of stacking, we run to a dish-washing machine .. after which the lads tidy up, then do whatever appeals to them, read, write, play scrabble or table tennis until ten o'clock bed. Of course Barbary will be bedded much earlier than that. You may care to see to it tonight yourself."

"I had every intention of doing so." Libby's voice was stiff. "Will Mrs. Dawson see to her after that?"

"Either Mrs. Dawson or I shall myself. You look surprised. Don't forget I'm parent-practising. Remember?"

"I remember." Libby had risen from the table and was crossing to a window to look out on the night.

It was richer than velvet, it was deep-piled plush. By her side now Pierce Hardway intoned, "The Blue Mountains nights are like no other nights. That—as well as the really deciding reason—made me come here."

"What was the really deciding reason?" It was only polite to ask, Libby thought.

"The cheapness of the land," he admitted. "It's a sad thing that it should be so, but it certainly suited me."

"Why is it cheap?"

"The fear of bush fires. The last one several years ago, an extremely severe one, scared the buyers away."

"But not you."

"It suited me," he repeated. "I got all this"—he extended an arm—"for a song."

"After which you worked on it, changed your name from Pearce to Pierce."

"Yes. I'll show you tomorrow."

She did not comment on that. She asked instead, "Why herbs, Mr. Hardway?"

"I was waiting for that. The answer is the same I should have given you when you asked 'why B.W.C.' It is : I, too, was once a ward."

"I begin to see light. You were adopted by people who had a herbary."

"Not at all. Just by a foster-mother who was all mother, and who had put in a small boy's cupboard on the day he arrived, tired and unsure, and, I remember, considerably frightened, a clove orange. What comprised a clove orange comprises to—well, in part, anyway—a herbary. In my own instance," he informed Libby, "I have plantings of clove-pink, of orris." He smiled faintly and reminiscently. "It just all led up from that."

She was barely listening to him. "Clove orange," she murmured. "That's why you named this place Clove Orange. And clove orange is what—is what—"

For she was remembering it all now, that smell of sunsoaked stone walls, mown hay, the breath of young flowers, the sharp reality of cinnamon, orris and cloves. A pomander ball. For the Meadows had called it that.

Grandmother, too, had put them in cupboards. Thin-skinned oranges fairly jammed with cloves, then rolled in orris and cinnamon. There had been one that Granny had said was fifteen years old. It had been very small and withered and hard, but it had still smelled like— why, like that scent tonight. In the built-in wardrobe. Swinging in the closet dark. So it had been a pomander ball hanging there—a clove orange.

"Certainly." She must have spoken her thoughts aloud, for he was inclining his head, agreeing.

Then he quoted :

"I'll make a clove orange to give to my darling,
I'll make a clove orange to please my delight,
And lay in her coffer to sweeten her linen
And hang by her pillow to sweeten her night."

He had taken out his pipe. He lit it slowly. "Eleanor
Farjeon, who knew clove orange too."

"Granny called them pomander balls," she proffered.
"That"—apologetically—"was why I was late tonight."

"I know," he intervened, "you were not here, you were
years ago."

"Fifteen years," admitted Libby. She said a little shyly,
"Thank you for the pomander ball."

The boys had finished the dishes and the tidying, she
could hear the first plop of ping-pong balls. Time, she
thought, for Barbary to go to bed.

She looked across at the little girl and saw she would
have no trouble. The child's head was nodding. It had
been a long day.

No trouble tonight, but what of tomorrow night? One
small girl among a parcel of boys, the only other representative of her sex a rather advanced-in-years housekeeper.

In the same way as he had read her before, he said
now, "There will be other girls. It will be a home, not
a house."

"With a mother?" She said it unthinkingly.

"Of course. The mother is the core." His eyes held
hers.

She went across to Barbary, but before she could take
the little girl in her arms, he took her. Mr. Clove Orange
did.

"She's too heavy for you," he explained.

As he walked easily with her down the passage to a
room next to Libby's he suggested, "No bath tonight, or
are you one of those obsessed cadets?"

"I'm obsessed enough to agree to no bath."

"Good for you." He gave a little puff of mock ex-
haustion. "Turn down the bed, please, this kiddo must be
stuffed with blue metal."

"She's stuffed with coriander and bergamot."

"And all the other things you gave her on the journey
up." He began unbuttoning the sleepy child, and Libby,

removing from Barbary's thin case a small nightie, took over the unbuttoning and slipped the little one into folds of flannelette.

"Why did you?" Mr. Clove Orange was asking her.

She understood that he meant her indulgence of Barbary ... a herb man *would* frown on that ... and she murmured rather weakly, "It was the real, not the seem things, I think."

At his raised brows she explained about the plane seeming to grow smaller, the mountain air seeming to be blue.

"So you gave her something actual in the form of pink ice-cream, chocolate sauce and nuts."

"How did you—" began Libby, then stopped, embarrassed. Of course he would know; the child had been sick all over him.

He smiled, a friendly smile that reached his eyes as well as his long, sensitive lips.

"Yes, of course I would know. Haven't I stopped at that same soda fountain every trip up?"

"Even when you were by yourself?" There was soft laughter in Libby's voice; she was relieved he understood.

"Why not?" he parried. "I, as well as you, can go back down the years."

"To eat pink ice-cream and nuts?"

"To yearn," he corrected, "like our moppet here, for the real and not the seem things. As a matter of fact"— looking levelly at Libby across the small cot—"I still do." There was a moment's pause as he tucked Barbary in, tucked expertly, Libby noted, then he asked, "Do you?"

A cold finger touched Libby's heart. The real, not the seem, things. The realness of family, a family that was, then wasn't any more. Mother, Dad, Paul, all gone. Gone in one year. Only the seem things, the remembered laughter, and the warmth, left in an image, a vision, a dream.

The man had left the other side of the cot to come to Libby's side. His eyes were gentle, sympathetic, they invited tumbling words. How easy if she could only respond. How *emptying*. But she couldn't. She felt she never would. She felt herself withdraw, hold her pain tightly to her as she warded him off with a cool, uninterested, "I'm afraid I can summon up no fellow feeling, Mr. Hardway. I was not an orphan, nor was I a ward."

He understood at once, he recognized a rebuff, and he bowed slightly. The gentleness had left him. "Are you finished with the child?" His voice was almost terse.

"She—she didn't say her prayers. I'll say one for her." But standing trembling there Libby could only murmur, "God bless."

They put out the light and went back into the common-room. Libby watched a spirited bout of table tennis, a round of Scrabble. She also watched the clock.

Before the hand reached ten, when Mr. Clove Orange had said the boys went to bed, she went to bed herself. Mrs. Dawson had already gone, having first performed a round of goodnights. But Libby chose a moment when everyone's attention was on something else to slip from the room *without any goodnights*.

She closed her bedroom door behind her, ashamed at her bad manners, but too tense to go back to right the wrong. The seem things, she was thinking emptily again, the dear days so irrevocably gone.

She crossed to the window and flung it up, hoping to find a balm to the spirit, even a herbal balm, in the night air. But she had forgotten how crisp mountain night air could be, and she closed the window again. Edgily she undressed.

Then, as she hung up her clothes in the closet, it stole on her again, that sense of sunsoaked walls, mown hay, young flowers.

She searched around the cupboards, and found it at last. The clove orange. The pomander ball. It was tied with a ribbon and it swung gently in the closet dark. It was little and hard, by its smallness and firmness about half as old as Barbary, she judged with a smile. She pressed down her nose to sniff the cinnamon and orris.

"I'll make a clove orange to give to my darling," she said softly. She took the pomander from the cupboard and hung it beside the bed. "To sweeten her linen, to sweeten her night."

She switched off the light and turned back the rugs.

Almost at once she felt herself uncoiling, felt her tension ease. Somewhere in the big house a clock chimed, a door closed, a window came down, a boy coughed. Libby slept.

She woke early, but she woke refreshed. For a while she just lay quietly, not wanting to disturb anyone in the house, but soon her inactivity irked her, and seeing a first pale ray of sunshine beginning to butter the sill of her window she got quietly up and crossed to look out.

The bush out of which the farm had been carved still hung on to its night shadows, but in the cleared spaces around the herbary there was the same primrose light as the beams now slatting into her room. It lit up the features of Clove Orange with a clarity not noticed on her arrival yesterday, so that this time Libby did notice, and she gave a soft cry of delight. Now she understood why it was Pierce, not Pearce. The man had literally pierced the thick bush, pierced and carved it, carved this from it, this quite perfect collection of plantations, propagation houses, pastures, tool depository, machine shops, barns, all so meticulously laid out it could have belonged to a model farmyard set and not to real life. Charmed with the planned patchwork quilt arrangement of it, the complete symmetry, Libby dressed quickly, peeped in to see if Barbary slept—and Barbary did—then hurried from the house.

It was crisp as an apple outside. She supposed that the Blue Mountains mornings would always be apple crisp;

her own hills of home in New Zealand had been sharp
and bright as pippins. She took a deep ecstatic breath,
then ran down a path to explore.

Stone fluted the edges of the path, hand-cut stone
that must have been delved and dragged from the blue-
grey bush, a bush now calling out to Libby to come and
see, see the weird, wonderful things that she knew that
only Australian bush has, trees with bark hanging like
ribbons of a maypole instead of autumn-bared boughs,
birds that laughed at you and soft-eyed animals that
carried babies in a pouch. The Blue Mountains were full
of these, she had been told, of bower birds who pick-
pocketed everything that was blue, of lyre birds who
sang every song that has been sung, but Libby knew that
first she had to examine the herbary, so, wide-eyed, she
did.

Many of the herbs she recognized, some of the low-
growing ones behind the stone edging she knew as thyme,
chives and hyssop, behind them the medium-sized mint
and marjoram, at the back the taller angelica, rosemary
and sage. But many more she did not know, though it
was easy to guess that that warm pungency that came
from a bush could belong to no other than peppermint,
that that fragrance redolent of sleepy days and bumbling
bees, although it was a different variety from the garden
variety with which she was familiar, was lavender.

She paused under a vine-hung lattice to peep into one
of the long iron sheds. It could only be *his*, she thought
with unwilling respect, only Mr. Clove Orange's "shop."
Where else would tools have hung so neatly, or leaned
so erectly against swept walls? She saw the careful
arrangement of sledgehammers, crowbars, crosscut saws,
scythes and sickles, and knew that only a man who had
had to earn all this, had had to pierce his way through
a wilderness with sweat and callouses, could have hung
and placed everything with such pride. In her heart she
had to admire his application, but, stubbornly, she dismissed it as too careful, the man himself as too meticu-

lous. Cut and dried and routine, as she had flung at him.
But one thing she could not dismiss : the essential man-
aroma of the "shop"—old leather, sawdust, creosote, toil.
A pungent, honest smell. The very essence, and this time
she admitted it freely, of Pierce Hardway himself.

A little confusedly, confused at her own tumbling
feelings, Libby turned to the sunlight again.

But not for long. The group of propagation houses
attracted her attention, and she went across. The ones
with the cut bush roofs were open for her inspection, and
she passed by. the benches of tiny seedlings, some no
longer than matchsticks, wishing she could sort out the
different varieties. Evidently they presented no puzzle
to Mr. Clove Orange, for they were not tagged, and
one section certainly needed no tag, even for Libby.
Garlic, she grimaced.

Beyond the bush houses were the glasshouses. Here
would be the more delicate, or perhaps exotic, herbs.

She peeped through a window into the greenish gloom,
then, to her satisfaction, saw that one of the doors was
actually unfastened. So Mr. Clove Orange was not so
perfect after all, she glowed. Also . . . wasting no time . . .
she would be able to go inside.

For the next ten minutes she forgot everything in the
green enchantment of the heated interior; it was like
entering a different world. This time the boxes of cut-
tings were carefully labelled. She rolled off the names
with delight. Balsam, eau-de-cologne mint, a section of
bare sticks tagged Artemisia abrotanum, with, in
brackets, "lad's love." She giggled to herself. She felt
sure that someone other than Mr. Clove Orange managed this section, for she could not imagine Pierce Hardway adding that. Probably the herb baron had passed
this glasshouse over to one of his subordinates, probably
he did not bother even to supervise, even to enter.

The next moment she knew that that supposition was
very wrong. In a clear, angry voice, clearer because of
the complete emptiness, save for the boxes, of the pro-

pagation shed, a voice, *his* voice, demanded, "How in tarnation did you get in?"

She turned and saw him at the other doorway—the herb baron. He came striding down the green gloom towards her and she saw that he was quite furious, really enraged. Could this be the same man who had gathered a little girl into his arms and crooned, "There you are, Princess, sweet as an apple again?"

Instinctively, in the face of rage, in the voice of anger, Libby withdrew a few steps, and at once Pierce Hardway stopped short. The fury was wiped out, and a half-shamed, almost little boy look took its place. *If* this man could look "little boy," she thought.

"I'm sorry I startled you, I didn't mean to."

"Shouting generally startles people—unless they have learned to expect it in a person. I hadn't." She spoke in a ruffled manner, for she was ruffled. "And of course," she added, "I won't be learning."

"Meaning you won't be here long enough to learn?"

"Yes."

"I'm sorry if you are thinking that."

He sounded almost as though she was thinking the wrong thing, which, of course, she wasn't, for, Barbary permitting, and it appeared by Barbary's angelic slumber this morning she would permit, Cadet Libby Meadows would be gone from Clove Orange long before lunch. However, he must mean he was sorry about the shouting at her.

He did not explain—only explained his wrath.

"It's very important that these glasshouses are locked every night, temperature has to be strictly controlled."

"Has my entry upset it?" She spoke coolly.

"Well, it hasn't helped it," he answered equally coolly. "However, it was the possibility of the door opening on its own accord through being insecure that really alarmed me. This stuff"—he waved his arm—"is in its infancy, it can't take a sudden temperature drop."

"Is it valuable?" she asked.

"Not at all, except for its unavailability. It's unavailable because it's not indigenous. In here I am endeavouring to bypass that."

"I wouldn't have thought," Libby said pertly, "that lad's love would call for such tender attention."

He came back blandly, "Would you not?" and Libby did not feel so pert.

"By his carelessness young Lennox could have been the cause of the loss of every one of these seedlings," Pierce Hardway went on. "Oh, yes, it's Lennox who does the closing-up each night. I'll have some words with that feller." He had crossed to a house phone and taken it up. He said crisply into it, "Send Lennox over to number three. *At once.*"

As he put down the phone, Libby said stiffly, "Couldn't it have waited? The child might have been eating his breakfast."

He looked levelly at her.

"One: he is not a child. Two: it could not wait. A reprimand, like a tender word, should never be delayed."

"Three?" asked Libby quickly, for she found that her glance had to slide away, slide away from that *too*-level look.

"Three," he said laconically, "he is not having breakfast."

"Is it too early? Or is it too late?"

"It is the breakfast hour, but this morning the meal is not ready. That's what I came out here for, Miss Meadows, to enlist your help. When you did not open up at my knock on your bedroom door, I took the liberty of looking in your room, and when you were not there I knew, unless you had run away, and it would have to be run, for your car had been garaged and the garage locked up, that you would be examining the herbary. So"—peering out to see if young Lennox was in sight and frowning because he wasn't—"I came searching for you."

"To tell me—" prompted Libby, but he held up his

hand, held it in the authoritative way of men of authority.

"Later," he said.

Young Lennox . . . Libby remembered him as definitely difficult . . . had come at last into the glasshouse. He looked apprehensively at Hardway and started at once into a babble of explanations.

As he had halted Libby, Pierce Hardway halted the boy.

"You knew how important it was to double-check the doors? No, no long account, Lennox, simply yes or no."

"I—"

"Yes or no."

"Yes," muttered Lennox.

"And you didn't double-check?"

Before she could stop herself Libby came in, "Mistakes can be made."

In such a low voice that only she, Libby, who stood nearer to him than Lennox, could have heard, he said, "You've just made one, Miss Meadows. Keep out of this, it's not your affair."

"I—" But she got no further. He turned from her and turned on Lennox again. There followed a brief but piercing harangue . . . that art of verbal attack, thought Libby bitterly, and not his triumph over the bush must have given him his name . . . then just when she and obviously Lennox expected the worst, he said, almost mildly, "All right, I'm done, get back to the house. And how is breakfast going?"

"N-not as w-well as when Mrs. D-Dawson g-gets it." Young Lennox was decidedly shaken.

"I have no doubt about that. Very well, Jim, don't stand there, get back and help."

Jim Lennox needed no second word, he turned and ran to the main building.

Libby simply stood and gaped.

A minute went past. In that minute Pierce Hardway lit a pipe. "By now," he drawled, "you must have gath-

ered that Four : Mrs. Dawson is not on deck this morning."

"She's ill?" Libby queried.

"Yes, occasionally she gets these attacks. My knock
on your door that was unanswered was an S O S."

"Can I help now?"

"No, on second thoughts it might do the youngsters
good to fend for themselves on this occasion. In which
case we won't return to the house until it's all over, that
is if your stomach will hold out."

"I'm not hungry," she assured him.

"And you wouldn't be, either, in the mess they've
probably created. What about Barbary?"

"I think she was very tired last night, probably she
will sleep well into the morning."

"Good. I'll show you around, give you an idea of
Clove Orange. After that it might be safe to return to the
house for a civilized cup of tea."

"What about Mrs. Dawson?" she asked.

"She would sooner wait for civilization as well." Before
Libby could think of any other protest he put light, indifferent fingers under her elbow and veered her out of
the glasshouse, carefully locking it behind him.

There followed one of the most fascinating hours that
Libby had ever known.

First there was the "physic garden" where herbs connected with potions and salves were grown.

The "bee corner" was thick with bergamot and budd-
leia, both beloved by the busy honey workers, while the
"scented garden" had every ingredient needed for pot-
pourri and sweet sachets. Each herb had its legend and
this man knew every one. Libby listened with fascination, drinking in every word.

The bread-and-butter herbs followed. "Bread-and-
butter in two ways," related Pierce Hardway. "They
compromise my bread-and-butter and they go well on
bread-and-butter. I'll show you when we return to the
house."

Next came the drying sheds, the packing sheds, the packaging sheds. "We do the whole thing," he nodded, "even to our own printing." As sounds issued from the house he added, "It looks as though they've fed themselves. Do you feel fit enough to return to the ruin?"

"I could do with a cup of tea," Libby admitted. She added politely, "Camomile or peppermint will do."

"You'll have Indian or China" he promised. "I grow herbs and I add herbs, but I don't live on them. I'd have liked you to see our bush beyond, but that can wait. All right, we'll find out the worst."

The worst was not at all bad, for the boys had cleaned up fairly well after them.

"Where are they now?" Libby asked.

"The seniors would have started their day's work, the juniors would have gone off to catch the school bus—they attend the ordinary mountain school. Next week you must register Barbary." Before she could say it he said for Libby, "Though I forgot, you won't be here."

During the next ten minutes Libby tried hard to make herself useful, but not knowing the layout of things she was not very successful, and so it was Pierce Hardway who brewed the tea, who cut the plate of herbal sandwiches for Libby to sample.

They were delicious, they had a fresh flavour she had never tasted before, and when she asked about them he said, "You have to experiment. That one you're enjoying now is pennyroyal, and it goes well with mint."

"It's odd." Libby said it to herself but aloud.

"Yes, Miss Meadows?"

"You don't look it." At his raised brows she explained, "Herbs. They sound—well, delicate, aesthetic, and you—"

"I am not that? I agree. But toughness and delicacy can still be akin, Miss Meadows, they are very much like the reprimand and the tender word, remember? To be considered in the same breath."

But Libby did not wish to consider. She got up from the table, saying, "I'll see to Barbary."

"She's asleep. I looked in as we came down the hall."

He would!

"Then Mrs. Dawson—"

"Yes," he agreed, "you can help out there. You can take along a tray ... just tea, nothing else." For all his gift of service he had the tray ready before Libby could set it.

A little nettled, Libby asked, "Which room?"

"Third on the right. Shall I open the door?"

"Leave me something," she almost snapped.

As she went down the passage she thought she heard him say, "There'll be plenty, don't worry," but she could not be sure.

But a few minutes afterwards she was sure. Any truant idea she might have had in her mind as to the authenticity of Mrs. Dawson's illness was instantly dispelled. Mrs. Dawson was definitely ill.

"I get it every so often," groaned Mrs. Dawson. "Migraine. So sorry, dear."

"How long do the attacks generally last?" Libby was facing up to a very disagreeable fact, the fact that she could not leave this woman in a condition like this.

"Not long, and then, of course, my sister lives handy, so she comes along and takes over for Pierce and the boys."

"Oh." Libby was vastly relieved to find that there would be nothing to prevent her after all from leaving quite soon.

"Only," sighed Mrs. Dawson, "this time I think it's going to take longer."

"But your sister—?"

"That was what I was going to tell you. It's providence, really you arriving yesterday, Miss Meadows. You see Cora's gone off to her daughter's."

"And how far would that be?"— The next mountain

town, thought Libby, perhaps even less than that, perhaps just down the valley.

"Melbourne," groaned Mrs. Dawson. "Gone for a month. Oh, dear, I feel dreadful again!"

She closed her eyes in distress, but opened them a moment to flick gratefully to Libby, "It's providence you being here, my dear. At least now I can relax."

Libby did the usual migraine things, pulled the blind, cut out the noise by shutting all the doors that led towards Mrs. Dawson's room, dipped a handkerchief in weak cologne and placed it on her forehead. Then she did the most important migraine thing of all, she left the sufferer alone.

She came back to the kitchen, seeing on her way if Barbary still slept—and Barbary did—then she went rather nervously down the passage and pushed the galley door.

To her relief the room was empty. Evidently Mr. Clove Orange was superintending his herb business, yet it was not such a relief in a way, for in several hours the workers would stop for lunch, and she apparently was supposed to feed them. Hard enough with ordinary victuals, but in a herbary presumably you would be expected to add herbal touches, and what touches went with which, for instance did tarragon complement—

"Not expected." A square of paper was propped on the working bench beside a collection of bottles. Underneath was suggested, "Just go ahead."

It was uncanny, she thought a trifle hysterically, how he anticipated everything.

Curiously she turned over the bottles. They were quite charmingly packed and labelled; if she had been a housewife she would have been tempted to try their fragrance and flavour. There were even suggestions as to use included in old curlicued print. "Coriander: Try with marmalade." Then—"Rosemary: A touch with stews."

What was for lunch? She opened the fridge door and

saw that Pierce Hardway had left out the doings. Easy
enough, she saw. Sausages, a positively huge platter of
sausages, but then they were a huge hungry family. She
went to the large range and saw that he had placed a
great grid in readiness. It appeared she had nothing to
do except place them on.

A little let down, she wandered round the kitchen,
picking up things and putting them down. But when she
picked up the large, illustrated recipe book from the
shelf she did *not* put it down. It was titled "Out of the
garden," and it was quite fascinating. But as well as
fascinating her, it did something else. As with that
pomander ball, that clove orange, hanging in her closet,
its sunny airs bringing back fifteen years, the pages of
the book performed a similar magic, but in ingredients
instead of fragrance, in the names of dishes that came
nudging, if faintly, at Libby's memory. Distantly, indeed
so far off Libby could not recapture any particular
moment, a recognition stirred.

Rosemary Snow, for instance. Where? When? Beneath
the name and before the recipe Libby read how Rosemary Snow once had been "a pretty conceit."

Angelica Tea. The author now asserted that this herb
in ancient folklore had heavenly associations.

Crystallized Borage. Borage? But of course, *borage*.
Five-pointed Madonna-blue stars growing in Grandpa's
farm in New Zealand, Grandma sugaring the flowers for
a treat for small Libby and smaller Paul. Almost unaware of movement, of anything around her, Libby
crossed the room to sink down on a window box . . . to
remember.

The four of them had been complete then, she remembered achingly. Six, with the grandparents, but that,
of course, was different. The two grans had gone on
because that is the pattern of life, the design for old age.
But Mother and Dad had been comparatively young,
while Paul—Paul— Oh, why did it all have to happen,

why? All those lovely, lovely times gone, gone forever. Everything finished and gone.

The tramp of young feet did not penetrate her absorption. It was only when his voice, Pierce Hardway's voice, remarked astringently of the book in her lap, "I suppose we should be flattered that you were carried away with our brain-child so much that you forgot that men also live on food as well as words, but I'm afraid, at the moment, anyway, that a fried snag would be a better offering to an empty stomach," that she looked up.

She came fumbling out of the past to the present to find him standing in front of her, behind him a positive army of boys.

"F-fried s-snags?" she stammered.

"Sausages." His voice now was terse.

"Oh, I know that, of course."

"Then perhaps your excuse is that you don't know how to cook them?"

"But I do."

"Then—?" He looked so cool, so judicious, that Libby's resentment flared.

"Has there to be an excuse?" she asked.

She did not look at him as she said it, she was quite disgusted with herself. For a third time she had let him down, let down Clove Orange, once with Barbary's bilious attack, twice with this morning's non-response to a breakfast S O S and now with no lunch prepared. Oh, how could she have forgotten that at twelve o'clock young stomachs, and older ones, demand to be refilled? He had left everything in readiness, she had only needed to place the pan on the fire. Nothing else. She bit her lip in annoyance, but was more annoyed a moment later when she felt her lids prick in a familiar fashion. Oh, heavens, she was going to cry!

Quick as she was in turning her glance away, Pierce Hardway was quicker in swirling her out of the French window. She heard him call something to the boys and heard them respond.

She felt his fingers under her arm as he impelled her down the stone path, and reaching the end of the path into the bush. He walked her until they came to a flat rock, then he pushed her down beside it. Pushed her gently. He took out a large handkerchief and pressed it on her. "The usual things," he directed, "a good cry, a good blow."

She handed the handkerchief back to him. "I don't want to now, thank you, and even if I did I've messed things up enough since I've been here without messing your handkerchief as well."

"Don't worry about that. The way we're going, or I should say the way Mrs. Dawson's going, *you'll* be handling the laundry, Miss Meadows."

Libby did not argue that she would be gone from Clove Orange before laundry day could come round, she simply said humbly, "I picked up the book and I forgot the time."

He had taken out his pipe. "That," he agreed, "seems the case, but I think"—more keenly—"there's a little more to it than that."

Now he was reaching out to her again, she knew, as he had reached out before, silently offering his understanding, his help, but once again Libby felt herself instinctively withdraw.

"It's a very fascinating book," she evaded.

"So much so that you cried?"

"I didn't cry."

"No?" He tapped at the pack in his pipe, loosened it, relit the pipe. "Yet there were tears," he stated.

"I—I was disgusted with myself, not even able to put the boys' dinner on the range."

"Mine, too. So"—keenly again—"that made you weep. You know what, Miss Meadows?" He waited, and Libby saw it was for her interrogation.

"What?" she obliged.

"You're a liar. It was not the sausages that you forgot that wrung your heart, was it?"

"My heart was not wrung." She said it deliberately, she was having trouble with a trembling lip.

"Look, I'm not nosing, I'm trying to help. Miss Meadows . . . Libby—"

At her name she looked quickly up and saw his eyes looking down on her, and they were so kind that the foolish tears pricked again.

Brokenly, in spite of that determination, she murmured, "The recipe book took me back."

"Back where?"

"To fields of blue borage. Grandfather had borage, and Grandmother made sugar petals for us—I mean for me."

His eyes were a little narrowed now, he was considering her. Libby went quickly, too quickly, on.

He stopped her by asking, "Where was this?"

"New Zealand."

"Then you were an Enzedder."

"Yes, we—I was."

The pipe was being attended again. "Then undoubtedly you would be a natural with herbs. The Enzedders are, they have fine gardens. Was it the crystallized borage that brought it all back?"

He did not mention the tears, and Libby was grateful for that. "Everything in the book kept ringing bells," she admitted, "just as the pomander ball did last night. It is"—sincerely—"a beautiful book."

"We all wrote it—Mrs. Dawson, the boys. I did myself. Then we printed it on our own press. It's sold well."

A silence fell between them. Libby broke it by reading aloud from the book. "Balm Delight," she said.

"That was Tessa's contribution, she insisted on being included."

"Tessa?" So there had been a female before Barbary.

"Tessa from Hoon Hay."

"Hoon Hay?" she echoed.

"Yes, you must have seen it." He shrugged. "It would be impossible not to see Hoon Hay."

As she did not comment, he commented himself.

"Tessa is a cross-current and a contradiction," he half-smiled. "For a young woman who knows with an almost male resolve where she wants to go and is determined to get there she can be surprisingly female at times. I would never have expected Balm from her, more Tarragon sauce, something with pungency and bite."

"But what is Hoon Hay?" asked Libby.

"You ask that?" he disbelieved. "An Enzedder?"

"Hoon Hay." She said it reflectively, experimentally. Then her face lit.

"Of course. Of course!"

Hooning the hay. How often Grandfather, who had been a New Zealand Scot, had said that. But this was Australia, not New Zealand, not second Scotland, so what was Hoon Hay here?

"In this neck of the woods it's the name of a house on the hill," Pierce Hardway told her. "Though that's not quite correct, this house is a small castle."

"Its owner came from New Zealand?"

"From either the first or second Scotland," he nodded, "for I would say that 'hoon hay' is not an Australianism."

"It's lilting," she said in instinctive defence, and he grinned.

"That's the way, Miss Meadows, always fight back, it's better than tears."

"Who," diverted Libby, "is Tessa?"

"She is a member of that castle on the hill." With the words he had impelled Libby to her feet again, hoisted her on top of instead of just against the rock.

"Look through the trees," he directed.

She peered through the grey-blue gums, seeing nothing at first but fleecy sky caught between the leaves, then she glimpsed something else caught there. A corner of a rose-pink edifice, a very beautiful, almost a magnificent edifice. The castle Mr. Hardway had just told her of? Hoon Hay?

She could not see very much of it, but what she saw

was almost breathtakingly lovely. Rose-pink timbered walls, a gracious dome of Mediterranean blue, mullioned windows set in almost as though they had grown there, flowing lines, elegant air, a sense of inbred pride.

"Hoon Hay?" she asked aloud this time.

"Yes."

"Why didn't I notice it before?"

"That's easy, the bush is very thick down here in the valley, only where the foliage clears would Hoon Hay rise up. Again, the colour of its dome would merge into the sky."

"Has the house been here long?" she asked.

"According to its patriarch it came just after the mountains came," Pierce laughed.

"Why do you say that?"

"You know what I mean." He shrugged. "Owners invariably claim a great deal more for their particular roof tree than could possibly be true."

"I didn't mean that, I meant why do you say patriarch?"

"Because that's what Julius Abberson is, a patriarch, and that's what Hoon Hay is, a patriarchy."

"And this castle-member Tessa? I mean Miss Abberson? Or"—at a look in his face—"is she that?"

"Everyone," Pierce Hardway replied laconically, "who lives in the aura of Julius Abberson becomes an Abberson, like it or not."

"Do any of them not like it?"

"Yes. Tessa. That's why—" He stopped, grinned slightly, then began attending his pipe again.

Libby looked back to the house, or what she could see of it, and what she could see was even more beautiful at a second look.

"Before I go back to Sydney I must have a closer view," she determined to herself, but aloud.

"That," interrupted Pierce Hardway, "brings me to a subject that we must discuss."

"My leaving?"

"*Not* leaving. Mr. Perkins rang through this morning. On no account are you to return to H.Q. until—"

"Until Barbary settles. I knew that."

"Until Mrs. Dawson is completely recovered," he corrected her.

"But that could take quite a while, I know these migraine attacks. Besides, you've told me that you're more or less self-sufficient here."

"Just now we have to be more," he reminded drily. "In one day we've had to get our own breakfast and lunch."

"Oh—lunch." She remembered it too late. "Will the boys still be waiting?"

"They will not. They will have fended for themselves, as they fended this morning, been quite pleased about it as a matter of fact as it will give them less time in the packing sheds and fields, for although they like their work, nor do they object to a later afternoon start."

"Then," endeavoured Libby, "there's no real reason for my staying. You've already stated that you're sufficient parent for Barbary."

"There is Mrs. Dawson to keep you."

"She could stay elsewhere."

"There is no elsewhere, except her sister's, and her sister is in Melbourne."

"Then someone could come in and look after her."

"But that's what must be avoided," said Pierce Hardway, "for that someone, as soon as she heard of the opportunity, would be Tessa, of course."

"Tessa up there?"

"Yes."

"And you don't want Tessa?"

"I don't particularly care," he shrugged, "but Mrs. Dawson emphatically doesn't want her, and believe me, the equanimity of a cook is a very important thing. She does not want, and will not have, Tessa. Prostrate though she is, I believe she will make a painful effort to tell you that should you suggest it. Also"—an edged smile—

"though it would take more than a herb baron, *your* title, Miss Meadows, to upset the Abberson design, the patriarch, too, would be unamused."

"What design?" asked Libby.

"Julius Abberson's design for Abberson marriage. Tessa Abberson is to marry Peter Abberson." Pierce added finally, "Full stop."

"Who is—" But Libby refrained from asking "Who is Peter Abberson?" If she remained here, and it appeared from the Chief's message she was to remain here for a while yet, she would soon find out.

"Why would Tessa want to come?" She found she had to ask one more question after all. The pink-washed walls of the beautiful house on the mountain top made her wonder how anyone could want to leave such a place, even for Clove Orange.

"Because," said Pierce Hardway simply, "she wants to marry me."

CHAPTER THREE

LIBBY was silent as they made their way back to Clove Orange again. Although she noticed the rugged features that had changed Pearce Hardway to Pierce, the jungle growth of bush, the tortuous tangles of palms and sapodillas, the coiling ropes of liana, she only noticed with abstraction. Even the exquisite wild orchids and the delicate violets passed her by, while a snake asleep on a rock only brought from her an idle, "Will you stop and kill it?" Her mind was on other things.

"No." Pierce's response was instant. "Why should I? It's minding its own business; I'll mind mine."

That could have been one for her, Libby thought; the things she was thinking were not her business. But even admitting this she still could not stop herself from mulling over what Pierce Hardway had just said: that the girl, Tessa Abberson, wanted to marry him.

Yet why not, Libby conceded unwillingly at last, a covert look at him emphasizing as well as the height, leanness and strength, the sensitivity of the profile and the mobility of the long mouth. There was a levelness about him, too, she had never encountered before, a solidity, a sense of purpose.

"Well, had a good look?"

Libby started uncomfortably and mumbled something indecipherable.

"If that's a denial, if you're trying to say you were not looking, it's another lie."

"Another?"

"You said previously," he reminded her, "that you were only crying over sausages that were not put on."

"We finished that subject."

"You might have. I have barely begun."

"It's none of your business," she muttered.

"Like our snake, eh? If that's so, then my appearance should be none of yours, and yet you've been looking at me for the last five minutes. Why?"

"I can see now," said Libby coolly, "why you were called Pierce and not Pearce."

"This jungle." He nodded to the encroaching valley around them.

"No, you. You dig and delve for answers, don't you? You probe."

"As I just said, Miss Meadows, I've barely begun." He lifted up a branch for her to pass under. "You've been thinking about Tessa Abberson wanting to marry me, haven't you?"

"No. I mean—well—" Libby finished with deliberate disinterest, "why shouldn't she?"

"I agree. I see no reason why anyone shouldn't consider me a fair to average matrimonial bid. I'm pretty well established, I'm old-young, which, for a young lady, I have been told, is a very attractive age, and I'm not quite repulsive. You concur?"

"I'm not interested," Libby said heatedly. Really, this man—!

"Lie the third," he commented mildly. "That five-minute speculation was no disinterest." As she did not comment he said, "I won't tell you why Tessa has her claws into me. Either Mrs. Dawson, or even Tessa herself, will probably tell you that. Anyway, there's no time now, we're through the bush and home again. I see the boys have gone back to work, so I'll cut off after them."

"You haven't eaten," she protested.

"Neither have you. Get yourself something. Mrs. Dawson, too, though I doubt if she'll take it."

"But you—"

"We're rather busy, so I'll grab a mouthful down in the shed during the afternoon. Do you think"—he proposed a little diffidently, the sarcasm discarded—"you could possibly whip up something for dinner tonight?"

"You're giving me another chance?" She broke into an eager smile.

He frowned at that. "Don't be absurd, it's not your job to cook for this tribe, but all the same if you could—"

"I'm going to." Already her mind was experimenting with casseroles and goulashes, she knew the wherewithal would be there in plenty, for the deep freeze had been amply stacked.

"And don't forget," he tossed, "we have a child."

That floored her, for she had forgotten. She, a dedicated cadet, had actually not remembered that—

"I never forget," she flung testily.

He laughed as he left her at the door of Clove Orange, so she knew her cheeks must have been guiltily red.

First of all she went in to Barbary. The small girl was still asleep ... she must have been quite exhausted last night, either that or it had been the sleep of happy reunion ... but even as Libby watched the sleep became lighter, and almost at once the child sat up.

Libby was wise enough to know that Barbary's first words, "I'm hungry," established her as definitely and indisputably settled in.

"So am I, pet. Into the bath with you and after that we'll see what we can find."

"I'm bathed at night," Barbary explained.

"You weren't last night."

"I can't remember last night, I don't think I can remember ever except now."

Libby caught her breath in satisfaction; there was so much for Barbary that was better forgotten, or at least passed over for the present. Yes, she was certainly settled in. If only Mrs. Dawson was recovered, there was nothing, or nobody, to keep Libby here.

But, leaving Barbary to soak in the tub, Libby found Mrs. Dawson still prostrate, though the sufferer made a painful effort, as Pierce Hardway had anticipated she would, to direct Libby that on no account must Tessa Abberson be allowed in.

It was cruel to question Mrs. Dawson in such a sorry state. Libby herself had had such attacks at times and knew how out-of-the-world they rendered you, but still, smoothing pillows, doing the few things that could be done, she found herself asking, "But why, Mrs. Dawson? Why don't you want her?"

"Because she has her finger on him, and she's not the right one."

"He doesn't seem so emphatic about that," returned Libby, recalling Pierce's indifferent shrug.

Mrs. Dawson gave Libby a quick look, if migraine prostration permitted such looks, and said; "You've noticed something, too. He's never been just like this before."

"Just like that?"

"Like—like—" But it was no use, Mrs. Dawson shut her eyes and simply gave in. Libby knew that that was the best thing to do, though she would have liked an answer, she would have liked to have found out what Mr. Hardway had not been like before. Lowering the blind again, she tiptoed out.

Barbary was playing in the bath, but when she saw Libby she remembered at once how hungry she had wakened up.

"We'll get something the moment you're rubbed dry and dressed, honey. How about a surprise sandwich?" Libby intended to experiment herself with those charming rows of bottles.

Barbary, however, said she would like fish and chips, but later ate approvingly of the chervil and cheese that Libby spread on the nutty loaf she found in the big bin. When the meal was finished she did as the boys had done, simply put the dishes in the big automatic dishwater. This was one thing she did heartily approve of in the herb baron, his generosity with mod. cons.

With no washing-up chores to perform, the afternoon grew longer. Libby did some quick cooking arithmetic and decided that before the appointed hour of the insertion of tonight's casserole, or casseroles as it would have to be, in the huge range, she and Barbary could indulge in a walk.

The little girl, completely rested after her mammoth sleep, was eager to begin, so Libby took a quick peep at Mrs. Dawson to see if all was well, if the blinds were sufficiently drawn, then, taking Barbary's hand, went out of the main building.

"Where shall we go?" she asked. "Down to watch Scott in the packing shed?" Or was Scott still on the basil planting? It didn't matter, they could try both.

But Barbary ruled out either.

"Scotty doesn't want me," she said quite equably. "He said if I ever turned up when he didn't say so he'd spit on my knee."

That, thought Libby, would be another version of the herb baron's brotherly clip across the ears. She felt she could have reported to Headquarters quite safely that Barbary had come home.

"All right, we'll explore," she suggested, and the two of them went down the path that Libby had taken this morning to the glasshouses.

Because Scott might be working in one of the houses, and because Libby did not want any clips across the ears, or spits on knees, she decided to bypass the herbary and push again into the encircling bush. Not far, though. She was sensible enough to appreciate that even though Australian terrain appeared sparse compared to her own New Zealand, one never took chances, that its features were so identical that six yards away from a pinpoint, the pinpoint became no point any more.

"We'll just look round and examine the foliage," Barbary."

"I know what that is," claimed Barbary, "it's a little horse."

"You're thinking of foal. This is foliage—trees, bushes."

"Why didn't you say?" Barbary complained, then, in the same breath, "What's that?"

Her little voice was excited now, and Libby did not wonder. For from this angle the house on the mountain top, "Hoon Hay," at which Barbary was gaping, looked like some faerie castle.

"It is Mr. Abberson's home, dear," Libby said.

"Is it magic?"

The pink walls merging into the blue dome that merged into the blue sky and into the blue bush did make something magic of the place, and though Libby said, "No, dear," she was not quite convinced herself.

"Can we go closer?" begged Barbary.

"Not much closer, we mustn't lose our way. Besides, there's dinner to put on, and besides again, it's private property." But even as she said it Libby was hot behind Barbary who was climbing, fascinated, up the mountain towards the tall, pink castle.

So engrossed was Barbary that she forgot to ask of private property her inevitable, "What's that?" So well-slept, also, that she soon left Libby well behind, but after all, grimaced Libby, this was Barbary's first walk today and it was her own third.

"Not too fast, darling... Barbary, no farther... Barbary, not over the fence!"

It was too late. Barbary was over the railing that evidently separated Hoon Hay from Clove Orange, and was running up the slope towards the pink goal.

"Barbary... Barbary!" called Libby.

The last thing that Libby wanted to happen happened at that moment. Someone emerged from the near-perfect formal shrubbery surrounding the house and caught the little girl up in strong arms.

"You're arrested, Barbary," said a pleasant voice, "and herewith returned to your keeper." Bright eyes smiled at Libby, who had scrambled over the fence, too, by now, and a man, younger than Pierce Hardway, tall, supple, added, "Pardon that 'keeper,' but one glance told me I couldn't say parent." He smiled.

Flushed with exertion, Libby smiled back at him. "Thank you, but I wouldn't have been affronted. I am, in a way, you see."

"A parent?" He looked incredulous.

"I'm a cadet with B.W.C. You mightn't know of that."

"I do."

"That's nice." Libby beamed on the man.

"How can being a cadet make you a parent?" He was playfully tweaking Barbary's tow hair.

"Well, sometimes we double-up as housemothers."

"I see." He smiled brightly at her again.

"I'm sorry we trespassed," proffered Libby.

Barbary interrupted as Libby should have known she would, for Barbary never believed in hiding any knowledge she had under a bushel, "That's the Big Prayer, the Little Prayer is before you eat, sometimes it's aboutereceive and sometimes it's blessthisfood, but the Big Prayer is always tresses."

"Trespasses," interpreted Libby for the man.

"I gathered so. But you weren't trespassing, not really."

"But isn't this Hoon Hay property?"

"It is, but just now it's a sort of open house. We're preparing for our annual fête, and if you go farther up the hill you'll find quite an army of non-Abbersons getting ready with marquees and what-have-yous."

"Can we go, Libby?" begged Barbary.

"No, darling, we can't."

"But you'll come tomorrow." The man, who had walked down the hill again with them as Libby, carrying Barbary, retraced her steps, relieved Libby of the child as she climbed through the fence.

"I don't think so," Libby declined politely.

"But everybody comes, it's unheard of in these mountains not to. I gather you're from Clove Orange."

"Yes."

"Then you can be assured that Clove Orange will be there in full force. Ask Pierce when you get back."

"Who," questioned Libby, "shall I say asked me to ask?"

"Abberson," he replied.

"But you don't look it." The words were out before Libby realized it. She clapped her hand over her mouth. "Sorry."

"I don't look what?" He was smiling again, not at all put out.

"A patriarch."

"To be that I'd have to be a father, wouldn't I, and, unlike you with your house-motherhood, I can't claim even that remotely to being a parent."

"Then who— Oh, I'm sorry again." She looked contrite.

"That's all right. You're referring of course to Uncle Julius."

"Is he the—"

"The patriarch? Yes. Though oddly he, too, is not a parent, the situation is strictly avuncular ... that's an uncle situation, though, of course, you'd know."

"Yes. But the patriarchy?"

He smiled again. "That's Hoon Hay, and since Uncle Julius is its head I expect he must be the patriarch." He hesitated a moment, moistened his lips. "It's not really as ominous as it sounds, even though Tessa—" He stopped, gave a small shrug, then lifted Barbary across the wire into Libby's waiting arms.

"It was nice meeting you. I shall look forward to meeting you again tomorrow. Can I mark you down on my strawberries and cream programme ... oh, yes, strawberries and cream is one of the fête attractions and a must ... as the first dish with me?"

"Will there be?" asked Barbary, enthralled.

"For the grown-ups," he nodded. "Sun sugar for the small fry."

"I don't know that."

"Uncle Julius," the man informed her, "doesn't approve of fancy names. Would you know cotton candy, then? fairy floss?"

"Yummy!" sighed Barbary.

"Then you're booked, Miss Muffet, for a very big cornet."

"Pink or white?" anticipated Barbary.

Libby was pulling her away now. "Thank you for not chasing us off," she said.

"You were welcome. Can I mark you down on my programme?"

"I don't think I'll be here."

"You will. It's an Abberson decree." His smile was a little crooked.

"Yet not," suggested Libby, "as ominous as"—she paused—"Tessa says?"

"How right, Libby. It was Libby I heard from Miss Muffet here, wasn't it? I'm Peter Abberson and I look forward to tomorrow."

"Goodbye, Mr. Abberson." Libby took Barbary's hand firmly this time, and they started down the hill again.

Halfway there, where a sudden dip in the terrain contour cut the upper part of the hill—and Peter Abberson—out of the picture, someone stepped from the thick brush. Rather tall, very slender, red-haired, green-eyed. About the same age, Libby judged, as herself. An exceptionally lovely girl.

There was a large black dog with the girl and Barbary asked slangily, evidently measuring the girl up and deciding she might speak a similar language to one she knew, though never used with Libby: "Is your mutt a meat-eater?"

"Barbary!" Libby was annoyed. B.W.C. was very particular over its wards' behaviour, its wards' manner of address.

"No, he isn't, you're jake," drawled the tall girl back to Barbary, while to Libby, because she had stepped forward to apologize for Barbary, "It's all right."

"But it isn't."

"So says housemother. You know"—ruefully—"that rather appeased me." A short laugh. "How wrong can you be!"

"What do you mean?" asked Libby.

"House*mother*. You're as much a parent as—"

He also had spoken of parenthood, that nice young man she had just encountered up the hill. Libby half-glanced back, just a flick, but it was a flick nonetheless that did not escape the girl's sharp eyes.

"What did His Nibs have to say?" she drawled. "No, don't tell me. It was strawberries and cream. He signed you up for tomorrow. Peter is always perfectly Hoon Hay, it's in his blood. Personally"—a shrug—"I prefer apples—green, tart, clean."

In spite of her rather discouraging attitude Libby found herself oddly drawn to the girl. She was hard, but Libby strongly suspected it was not a deep-down hardness, more a veneer. Instinctively she found herself responding to the forthright manner. "I, too, prefer apples," she said.

The reply was not encouraging. "Well, it can't make two of us." The girl knelt down and began nuzzling the dog.

"Name of Friendly," she introduced to Barbary, "and strictly a biscuit-eater, except, on occasion, a little boy with mustard or a little girl with tomato sauce."

"I like tomato sauce," declared Barbary.

"Then you two have something in common." Libby, watching them, was glad that Barbary anyway was not to be excluded as she had been.

Barbary said cautiously, "Hullo, Friendly," and warily touched the broad head.

While she was so absorbed Libby took the opportunity to talk to the girl.

"Why did the word housemother appease you?" she asked.

"It sounded deep-bosomed and maternal, not a *femme fatale*."

"*Femme fatale?*" puzzled Libby.

"You."

"But I'm not!" Libby protested.

"No, you're not," agreed the girl, considering Libby. "And come to think of it that would never have appealed to Pierce. You're a blue-starred sprig of borage. Even eyes to match. He'd love that herby touch. He probably loves you already."

"What nonsense!"

The tall girl bent over and selected a stem of bittersweet then chewed on it reflectively. "It better be," she warned quite brazenly, "because he's marrying me. Perhaps"—a sidelong glance—"he mentioned that."

"Not exactly."

"Then he might have mentioned that I'm marrying him. It adds up to the same thing."

Libby said, "You're Tessa."

"Then he did speak of me," the girl smiled.

Barbary, who had very big ears for a little pitcher and who had not been giving Friendly all her attention, said judiciously, "I don't think you're suitable."

The girl narrowed green eyes on the child and retorted, "You know what, kiddo, I think the same about you."

Barbary digested this, experimented with the fascinating idea of marrying her new idol, then rejected it.

"He's terribly old. I'm marrying my brother."

"Good, for you having your future all settled, good for you having a brother."

"Haven't you?" It was Libby—politely.

"No. Instead I have the whole lot," the girl tossed impolitely, and Barbary, a little shocked even for Barbary, regarded her with speculation.

She must have decided that the answer was rather silly, that Tessa was like all grown-ups only sillier, for she turned her attention again to the dog. Friendly gave her cautiously extended hand a wet, warm lick, and all was well. The two went scampering through the bush, Libby calling after Barbary to take care and not get out of sight.

"Don't worry." Tessa was lighting a cigarette. "When I whistle Friendly will fetch her back."

As an afterthought she offered her cigarettes to Libby, but it was not churlishness, Libby felt, but self-absorption. As Libby refused, Tessa nodded of the refusal : "That, too, would put you in Pierce's company. He would refuse a cigarette as well."

"But he smokes a pipe."

"So you do notice him," Tessa commented.

"I've noticed that." How could she not have noticed, Libby thought, that slow-measured packing and tapping and lighting, that same patient deliberation that he showed with the boys. And, remembering yesterday, with a little girl.

She became aware that Tessa was regarding her closely now, green eyes narrowed almost to slits. What was wrong with her? Did she—could she think—

"I'm not interested in Mr. Hardway in any manner or form," Libby said stiffly. "You can take it from me that I'm only here because I've been so directed. Don't for a moment assume that I—well, that I intend—"

Her voice trailed off as quite suddenly—and very disarmingly—Tessa's stony face relaxed into a smile. From the smile grew a laugh, and presently they both were laughing.

"We should be the dogs, not old Friendly," Tessa submitted between giggles, "fighting over Pierce as though he were a bone."

"I'm not fighting."

For a moment the acidity returned to Tessa. "So you say. But girls like you can fight by remaining quiet and calm and demure. I only wish I had that art. But alas, I'm me."

"You're Tessa Abberson." Libby could not have explained why she announced the name, but Tessa's reaction was sharp and unexpected.

"Why do you say that?" she demanded.

"Why? Well—well, you are, aren't you?"

There was a pause. It was a lengthy one. An enigmatical one.

Then— "No," Tessa said, "I'm not."

"But you just told us that you had more than a brother, that you had—"

"The whole lot? I have. I have the whole lot of Abbersons. Brothers, sisters, cousins, aunts."

"And," included Libby with deliberation, "Uncle Julius."

"Yes, Uncle Julius."

There was another silence, longer than before.

Libby stole a look at the girl. She was extremely attractive even with sullen rebellion in her face. Rebellion—yet something else as well. Libby was too long associated with that something else not to recognize it at once. How many times had she met it in a child? Wistfulness. This girl was wistful, though she would probably never admit it. She was not entirely the flinty type that she wanted to appear.

"Tessa—" she said impulsively, aware of the wistfulness, wanting to help. Like Barbary with Friendly, she half-extended her hand.

For a moment she thought she was going to be rewarded with another uncaring shrug, a derisive laugh, but, almost as though she was at the end of her tether, at the end of something, Tessa turned and submitted tightly, "All right, I'll tell you. That's what you want, isn't it?" As Libby tried to protest, she went on jerkily, "If I don't tell you, someone else will, so here goes." She took a deep breath, then: "I'm marrying Pierce."

"You said that before."

Tessa followed on, "To get away."

"Away?"

"From Hoon Hay. From—him."

From Peter? From Julius? Libby did not ask it yet, but she did ask, "Why does it have to be through Mr. Hardway?"

"Geography," came back Tessa with a shrug. "There's no other eligible male in miles."

"You could try somewhere else." Libby had decided to talk in the same flippant strain as the girl, but she was unprepared for the quick, strained response to her airy words.

"I did try. I tried going away once. It—it wasn't a success." Suddenly all the hard flippancy had dropped away.

She looked so wretched that Libby's heart went out to her. "Tell me, Tessa," she said.

"It's a silly tale, really. I ran off to Sydney for a job." Her face twisted in memory.

"Did you get one?"

"Yes. And lost it. I should have expected that, I'd never been trained for anything. But it wasn't that that brought me back, it was—it was—"

"You were homesick," Libby said, and the girl flinched.

There was silence for a moment, then Tessa cried, "How could I be? How could I? It's not my home."

"You're Tessa Abberson."

"Only by name. At the same time as Julius Abberson accepted Peter as a ward, he took me in. Only Peter *was* an Abberson, distant, perhaps, but never a rank outsider like—like—" She bit her lip.

"I think," said Libby practically, as she had said with determined practicality many times to unsettled wards., "that you should be thankful, not resentful."

"It must sound like that—but you've never met Uncle Julius. He's a spider, a lovely silver spider. He spun his web and then he caught his flies. Peter. Me. A spider." She repeated it. "In a web."

"And yet," Libby dared,. "you love that web." She was looking up at the pink castle on the hill.

"I don't love it. I won't. I was revolted at myself when I came crawling back to it as I did. Why did I? Why?"

"Because you felt amputated away from it."

"But it was not my right to feel anything. I'd never belonged."

"Had you been told that?" Libby asked quietly.

In a flat voice Tessa said, "All my life."

There was another silence, longer than before. Libby's heart was reaching out to the girl now in sympathy and understanding. How could any man have been so starkly cruel to a child? So pitiless to tell her: "You don't belong."

"But still you were fed, sheltered, clothed." She said it as practically as she could to Tessa. Cadet words, she thought. B.W.C. stuff.

"Of course. That was the design."

The design. The Abberson design. Pierce Hardway had spoken of that. He had said that it would take more than a herb baron . . . "your title, Miss Meadows" . . . to upset the Abberson design.

"The design that you and Peter—" she murmured.

"Yes. That we marry. That instead of closing the Abberson book, which would have had to happen because there was no one to carry on, we would start another chapter."

"But did this chapter have to be with you, Tessa? I mean Mr. Abberson already has his blood tie in Peter."

"For twenty years," reminded Tessa tightly, "I had been trained, moulded, bent. You don't waste that."

Libby was quiet a while. Then: "It's too fantastic," she said.

"Yet true. Outwardly Julius Abberson took me in to be a companion to Peter, actually he wanted someone he had prepared himself for the Abberson future. But sometimes all the preparation in the world, all the bending and moulding doesn't produce the shape you want. I'm not the shape Uncle Julius wants, and I won't be. And I won't become an Abberson by marrying one. Not"—

bitterly—"that I could ever want to be an Abberson. Why, I—I—"

Libby thought with sudden discerning pity: "She protests too much."

"So," finished Tessa with challenge, "I'm marrying Pierce Hardway to prove all that."

"And what of Mr. Hardway?"

"He'll be doing all right," Tessa said airily. "I'm a worker, and Clove Orange can do with those. He hasn't got used to the idea as yet... at least he likes to give that impression... but he'll come round in the end."

"And Peter?"

"What about Peter?" Tessa's voice now was rapier-sharp.

"What is his attitude?" Libby asked.

"I don't know. How could I know? How could I know how an Abberson ticks?"

"From what you've told me about Uncle Julius," said Libby thoughtfully, "I think an Abberson might tick the same as you, you have the same stubborn streak."

She became aware that Tessa was looking at her oddly, almost strangely, her hand up to her throat. "I've always felt like that, too," she half-whispered. "I've always felt that I—that we—"

She straightened herself, brought the hand down again.

"Well, now you know the story," she said jauntily, "are you going to wish me luck?"

"To marry Pierce Hardway so you can still look up at the house you didn't have the strength to leave because you loved it... or loved someone there... too much?" Libby paused, then said, "No, Tessa, but I wish you happiness."

"So long as I get away," said Tessa broodingly, "it will be that."

She turned to the bush to whistle Friendly. As the dog and Barbary came bounding through the undergrowth she said rather gruffly to Libby, "Thanks for listening, anyway, I think it's done me good. Will I see you tomorrow?"

"I'd rather gathered you didn't want me around." Libby half-smiled.

"Around Pierce was the idea." Tessa had her cigarettes out again. "You can hang around me."

"Then that would be around Pierce, too."

"Smart girl," Tessa awarded flippantly. Then she said seriously, "But I would like to see you again."

She climbed the hill to the dividing fence, straddled it, and was gone without another word.

A moment later, Barbary now by Libby's side, there was a second whistle . . . an automatic whistle. By the fast-gathering shadows, and Libby had not noticed them before, a knock-off whistle. Oh, no, she thought.

Too late came the bitter realization that her cooking mathematics were going to come up with a wrong answer. That she had in fact no answer at all.

The casserole. She had forgotten all about it!

For the third meal today, and third times are provers, she had not remembered that boys—and men—must eat.

In short, she had flunked again.

As Libby and Barbary approached Clove Orange a delicious smell accosted them. For a despairing moment Libby believed that Pierce Hardway had left the packing sheds early to come across to see how the new cook was coping, then finding her not coping had taken over the reins himself. The thought was desolating. Libby decided she would sooner the scratchiest meal than an aromatic *pièce de résistance* dreamed up by him.

But, pushing the screen door of the gallery, she saw to her extreme joy that Mrs. Dawson was again at the helm. She wore a capacious white overall and she looked bright and fit. But then, of course, migraine was like that, a victim was down one moment, up the next.

"You're better, Mrs. Dawson. You were sleeping when we left."

"And I woke up fresh as a daisy. The tablets must have

reacted at last. One thing, migraine is like all sickness, after it's over you forget the distress."

"I feel terrible not being here to help you with dinner."

Mrs. Dawson gave a beatific smile and Libby knew she was like all cooks, she preferred to perform her culinary operations on her own.

Just as beatific herself at the turn of events, Libby asked, "What are we having, or is it a surprise?"

"It's bitsies of meat," informed Barbary, leaning over the table, "on little sticks."

"Skewers, pet. It's kebabs, a favourite with the boys. I thought I'd give them something extra seeing—"

"That I haven't." Libby looked ashamed.

"It's not your job. I add coriander usually, but today I'm trying chicory."

"The pudding smells of lemonade," sniffed Barbary appreciatively.

"It's lemon-scented custard, dear, but the lemon scent comes from a geranium leaf. There's a lot of varieties of suitable geranium, suitable for flavour I mean, each with a different fragrance. There's Clorinda, a pretty name, I always think, and there's Fair Ellen and Geranium Robert."

"I know him," acclaimed Barbary, "he went to the same school as I did in Sydney, and he used to pinch me. Pinch real hard. Here comes Scott."

The painful memory of the pinching Robert must have given her a punitive impulse. She promptly went across and pinched her brother. Judging by his squeak, she pinched sharply! He in return promptly clipped her ears, and a small family row emerged. Pierce Hardway, who had entered the room just in time to see the revenging clip, had Scott out of the room before Libby could take stock of it all.

But she was not long after him, knocking imperatively on his closed door, and when it was not opened for her, nor was she bidden to enter, she opened it of her own accord. Really, she was thinking indignantly, this Pierce Hardway is too high-handed altogether! He takes one look, makes a flash judgment, then punishes on that judgment. If Scott "clipped," then he certainly had good cause.

"You have no right to—" she began as she stood in the threshold, and then she stood surprised. Only Mr. Clove Orange was there.

"Where is Scott?" she blurted.

The brows above the cool eyes were raised. "Do you usually enter private rooms like this?"

"I knocked."

"Banged, you should say."

"You never opened up," she retorted.

"I'm not accustomed to responding to banged doors, Miss Meadows."

"I'm sorry." Libby said it with smouldering; knew the smouldering showed and didn't care.

"You're not, though, are you?" He was taking out his pipe, lighting it with his usual leisurely deliberation.

There was something about the unhurried action that made one feel inexperienced, and inexperienced she was not, rankled Libby, she was sure she had dealt with more young than had Pierce Hardway.

"You're quite wrong about Scott," she attacked, "Barbary started it all. I think she was pinching because of Robert." At his surprised look she added foolishly, "Geranium Robert."

The next moment Pierce Hardway was dealing with Libby with the same minimum effort that he had dealt with Scott. But instead of outside the room as in the boy's case he had Libby in the room, not just halfway through the entrance. He had her pushed down into a chair.

"Calm yourself," he advised.

"But Scott—?" she began.

"He has not been maltreated. That was what you anticipated, I remember, down in Sydney with Paul Sellers."

So he had not yet forgotten the Paul episode, Libby thought.

"He's not here," she remarked of Scott.

"He could be crammed in that filing locker. Why don't you make sure?"

"Don't be absurd!"

"Don't you, Miss Meadows. You burst in to exclaim over the boy and then exclaim when there's nothing to exclaim over. Tell me, what did you expect? A cat-o'-nine-tails in action?"

"I just wanted to explain that you had judged too quickly, that Barbary had—"

"Pinched her brother because of Robert. Go on, please."

Libby said faintly, "Geranium Robert. I think that's what started it. You see Mrs. Dawson was telling how the pudding she's made for tonight was lemon-scented custard, and how the lemon was really—" She stopped short. What a fool! He needn't have known she had failed a third time to produce a meal, forgotten that boys—and men—must eat. Mrs. Dawson certainly would not have bothered to inform him, and Barbary would have forgotten, but who had seen to it that he was told of the omission? The one who had omitted.

"I . . . that is . . . well, when we came back . . ." she stumbled.

"We?" He was trying to hide a little grin as he ostensibly attended his pipe, for her incoherence amused him, but Libby's eyes were down.

"Barbary and I."

"And where had you been?"

"For a walk. We had meant to return to make a casserole, not knowing Mrs. Dawson would wake up recovered, and then—well—"

"You're really trying to say, I believe, that as a cook to Clove Orange you're no great shakes."

"Yes," Libby admitted.

"Well," he conceded with a maddening benevolence,

"as I implied before, housekeeping was not expected from you. You're a cadet." A pause. "Or so I've been given to believe." There was an unmistakable note in his voice that invited challenge. Libby challenged.

"Given to believe?" she pounced.

"A B.W.C. cadet is supposed to have more common sense than you showed just now, that, by your angry presence here, you are still showing. What do you think I am, Miss Meadows, a boy beater? Don't you appreciate the fact that I've gathered enough data about Scott in the weeks I've had him here not to know that he would never attack, unprovoked, his small sister?"

"But you were so quick with him."

"I didn't want more pinching, which would undoubtedly have come from the enraged Barbary, but this time on account of Scott, not any Geranium Robert."

"Robert," explained Libby rather foolishly, "went to school with Barbary in Sydney." She asked, hoping to divert the focus from herself, for she was feeling rather silly, "Where is Scott?"

"Doing ten more minutes in the packing shed. Any objection?"

She thought that over and decided it was not a bad punishment for a clip across the ears—after all, Scott was fifteen to his sister's seven and should have restrained himself. Mollified, she asked next, "Will I reprimand Barbary or will you?"

He smiled slightly. "Whoever it is, we'll go easy, this pinching Robert suggested by Geranium Robert might have had long hurting nails."

"You mean you agree with me that Barbary didn't really intend to take it out on Scott?"

"Yes. But it's still not a case for applause and ice-cream, is it?"

Libby said, inspired, "I'll put her to bed instead of you putting her."

"Would that be a reprimand?"

"She has a crush on you. Though"—Libby remembered back—"she doesn't want to marry you, you're too old."

"Is that Barbary, Miss Meadows, or is it you? And how did this matrimonial conversation come up?"

"It came when we met Tessa."

"Ah, Tessa." He reached for matches to relight his pipe. "So you met Tessa," he said, and sat back.

From outside Libby could hear the clatter of dishes and she half-rose from the chair into which she had been impelled. At least, she thought, I can set the big table.

"It's the boys' job," Pierce Hardway interrupted. "As well as doing the chores after they do the chores before." He puffed out a weave of smoke. "How did you find Tessa?"

"Good."

"Good? Tessa?" He grinned.

"I mean I enjoyed meeting her."

"You needn't be so perfunctory, I know the lady well, remember. I repeat, how did you find Tessa?"

"I liked her very much."

"That's better. I do, myself."

A demon in Libby made her say, "That's rather to be expected before marriage, isn't it?"

If she had anticipated a denial of marriage, she was not given it.

"Yes," he agreed quite calmly, "in fact I would say that liking a person is as important as loving them."

A little out of countenance, Libby chattered, "Tessa told me about the fête tomorrow, and how everybody goes."

"Quite true," Pierce nodded. "I agree in this instance with the Julius law."

"Will you tell me about Julius Abberson?"

"I rather think Tessa must have told you herself; invariably she tells of nothing else."

"On this occasion she did include the subject of marriage," put in Libby slyly.

"That inclusion would be part of the other topic," he

came back drily, "her marriage as a means of Abberson escape."

"Marriage with you."

"With anyone available."

Yes, she had said almost that, remembered Libby, and suddenly feeling for Tessa the utter desperation that must have prompted her to talk as she had to a total stranger, she said to Pierce, "It's all untrue, of course, it must be."

"What Tessa said?"

"Yes."

"No, it's true. Well, basically, anyway."

"How basic?"

"Her adoption as a child by Julius Abberson."

"She didn't put it that way, she spoke of it as a web."

"Like all females she emotes. You did yourself over Scott just now."

"I don't think Tessa emotes," denied Libby.

"Which means you believe she is serious, which means then I must take her intention of marriage to me in earnest after all."

"But hadn't you? Mrs. Dawson seemed to think you had been different of late, not as you were before."

"What's this?" Pierce Hardway was looking at her in that level way of his. "Why the pumping? Are you gathering material for an article on the lovelorn for some woman's magazine?"

"You don't like women, do you?" she commented.

"I like little women—Barbary. If you can bear to leave the fascinating topic of the Abbersons for a few minutes I'd like you to hear that Mr. Perkins has two more little women in view for Clove Orange."

"That's splendid!" Libby, unable to resist the topic nearest her heart, began an enthusiastic conversation on a suitable wing, on a timetable, on how long after the next two could they take two more. She realized too late she had included herself in the exciting programme, decided it would only emphasize it if she now excluded herself, so let it pass. But she had flushed at her discovery, her hot cheeks told her so.

If he noticed, he did not comment, neither on the warm colour nor her self-inclusion.

As the bell rang for the evening meal he smiled, "I'm sorry I didn't satisfy your curiosity over the Abbersons, but I believe that's something that is better satisfied by you yourself. And now shall we satisfy Mrs. Dawson? Hearty participation is her chief satisfaction. And it's not at all hard, I can tell you, when it's kebabs."

Scott had returned from his extra ten minutes' work, and was seated beside his sister, who looked so contrite that Libby considered skipping a reprimand after all. Then she saw that Scott wore a substantial bandage over the small pinch, which was reprimand and more. Every time Barbary looked at it, her lips trembled.

"That cunning boy," Libby whispered, then surprised a certain smug look in Pierce Hardway's face.

"You!"

"Yes, I bound the scratch up. Why not? She wasn't going scot-free. A better punishment, don't you think, than you putting her to bed instead of giving the job to me?"

"Perhaps," admitted Libby, "yet perhaps not. Perhaps she didn't mean that you were so old after all, and deprivation would have been more punitive."

"You never said," he reminded her, drawing out Libby's chair for her, "whether that was your viewpoint or Barbary's. I don't refer to the punishment but to my age. My marrying age."

"I was only a listener-in to the matrimonial conversation. Hush! Grace."

William said it, William who had been responsible for more of Daddy Perkins' grey hairs than *tempus fugit*. Libby believed the pigments of colour would have come back if Daddy Perkins could have seen William now, surly, defiant William standing importantly up there delivering the blessing in a solemn voice. What was it this man Hardway possessed that he could dig down and come up with nuggets of gold? He was so wise, too. The bandage on the pinch and the pincher's drooped lip, for instance. It didn't seem right that he could be so knowing, not when he was untrained, child-untrained, as he was. But perhaps, being a future parent, as he had emphasized, he had studied the art.

"You're staring at me." He broke into her rumination. "Boys of this age could make a mistake and put it down to the same reason as Tessa's and Barbary's preoccupation." He smile slightly. "View to mat."

"Be quiet!" Libby took up a kebab in the way the others were taking them, by the end of the skewer. She bit into meat bits, bacon, pineapple and onion cubes, all fragrantly redolent of the chicory that Mrs. Dawson was trying out, and awarded, "Cordon bleu!"

"Chicory flowers *are* blue, you know," he nodded, "china blue petals on long spires."

"I only know chicory as something that goes with coffee."

"We'll have to educate you. After dinner, I think." As she went to mumble some excuse, he pointed out, "Tomorrow's the fête, and then probably you'll be gone."

Always it had been Libby who had been ready to leave, but now, calmly informed that her wish could be at hand, she sat a little dismayed. She found there was so much she wanted to stay longer for. The incoming two little girls and their settling in. The unfinished story up the hill. The charm of Clove Orange that was beginning to encompass her like the delicate herbs encompassed every dish that Mrs. Dawson triumphantly created. Even—yes, even Mr. Clove Orange himself. What made him tick, made him such an unusual man, for, like him or not, one could never deny that he was not of the accepted run of the mill. Finally, Tessa. In some odd way Libby felt an association with Tessa. It was absurd, of course, but she felt she would help the girl. However, she was going away, or at least would "probably be gone."

It was like having a book taken away before you had finished. More disappointed than she would have admitted, Libby put down her kebab.

"You just awarded it a cordon bleu," he reminded softly beside her.

"I know, but—"

He took it up by the skewer and passed it back to her. "Eat," he said. "You're not going yet."

"You!" she gasped. "How did you know what I was thinking, I mean—"

"You're transparent, Libby." He said her name quite naturally, and she wished she could accept it in the same way. "Everything about you cried out for a little longer, for the end of the story, for the happy ever after."

"Really, Mr. Hardway!" She was glowering at him.

"The young are watching," he warned. "Eyes down." As she complied he said, "We'll continue all this during our herb inspection."

"If I go herb inspecting that's what I expect," she retorted.

"And will get, I promise you." He gave a confirming nod.

Before she could thank him ... or not thank him ... and for the life of her Libby could not have said truthfully which, Barbary trilled, "Here comes the custard that smells of lemonade!"

He kept his word in the inspection that followed, there was none of the interchange that he had tossed during dinner.

He took her from the plantings ... illuminated at a touch of a switch so that if needed, for instance in case of frost or trespass, attention could be given ... to the drying, packing, bottling, printing and final presentation sheds. It proved a Once Upon a Time world, this world of herbs, and here was a man who could recapture the magic.

He told Libby how primitive man had wrapped his food in leaves to protect it from the ashes, only to discover what was the first rule of herb production: flavour.

His stories were fascinating. For each herb, he had an anecdote. Of chicory he reminded that Culpeper had promised that a handful of leaves boiled in water "drives forth humours," that someone else centuries before had said of angelica that it drove away "pestilent aires."

"And garlic?" smiled Libby.

"Bottom in *Midsummer Night's Dream* did not recommend it for sweet breath," Pierce smiled back, "but wait till you taste it in Mrs. Dawson's sausages in cider."

Basil was remembered in Keats' *Isabella and the Pot of Basil*, a rather grisly tale, not in keeping with the bush basil that Clove Orange went in for, small and sweet and flowered.

House after house they examined, the stories growing, the fascination pulling Libby in almost as though down here was the web, and not the castle on the hill, a web of fragrance and flavour and once upon a time.

Rosemary . . . "dew of the sea." Redolent of Tudor days, of the holy legend of the Virgin Mary throwing her robe over a rosemary bush while she rested, and the white flowers turning to blue.

"Most herbal flowers are blue," told Pierce, "even pennyroyal is lavender-blue." He was looking levelly at her, and Libby, remembering Tessa's accusation that even her eyes were blue-starred borage, flicked her own glance away.

She saw the printing works where the labels in delicate old type complemented the charming bottles and phials as they told the name of the herb and its suggested use.

Then there was cosmetic section. "Doing very well," reported Pierce, "except that most of the boys shy off, reckon it's sissy, so finally I have had to roster them. Perhaps we'll be able to inveigle the little women to help."

He added, dead-pan, but glancing remindingly at Libby, reminding her of the time she had called him a cheap employer, "At a fee." He asked Libby, "At what age does a young female put lavender lotions and wallflower soap before honey of roses?"

"Honey of roses! That sounds toothsome."

"Recipe: Take the white heels from a pound of red roses and put them in a stone jar, etcetera, etcetera. Well, I think that's about all." They had left the last house, and he was reaching for his pipe.

It was only a few yards to Clove Orange, but the moon had not risen yet and the way was dark. He put his fingers under her arm. They were warm in the cold mountain air.

"Thank you for giving me a tour of inspection," said Libby.

"Thank you for being so charmed. I'm rather like a parent over my herbs, I thrive on praise."

"Then there at least you do not have to practise for the future." At his raised brows she explained, "At being a parent. You already are."

"Father to mint, marjoram, lavender, rue, dill—"

"Lad's love," added Libby.

"But I'm not a lad."

No, thought Libby, you are old-young, which, for a young lady, is a very attractive age. Your words, Pierce Hardway.

They had reached the door of the house proper and he had kept his promise only to talk about his work.

For a moment Libby looked back at the perfect symmetry of the herbary setting, she breathed the air that she had told Barbary on their arrival here at Clove Orange was the very breath of heaven.

"All from a pomander ball," she marvelled softly, "hanging in a closet."

"And land going cheaply, land with good black soil, growing soil, herb soil."

"And years of piercing the bush, Pierce." She called

him Pierce as naturally as he had called her Libby earlier in the evening. But the naturalness did not last. She realized what she had said, and she blushed in the darkness. She always had blushed, it had frustrated her when she was younger, but she had never got out of the habit of it, and she had found the best way was to get right away, so, murmuring more thanks, she got away now. She bustled Barbary to bed, and it was quite a bustle, for Barbary, having slept well into the day, was not sleepy now, and Libby only got her there finally by promising an extra ration of fairy floss to what she was already promised from Peter Abberson at the fête tomorrow.

After bedding Barbary she went to her room, cheeks still pink. She was naturally a reserved, almost circumspect little person, even without Daddy Perkins' wise tuition to his young girl cadets always to be friendly with patrons but in a reserved, circumspect manner. "We have proved," had tutored Mr. Perkins, "that this sets a desirable standard and assures respect."

Whatever her use of his name had set or assured to Pierce, Libby did not know, but she knew it certainly confused her own standard. Why had she not stuck to a formal Mr. Hardway? Why had she relaxed with this man?

She went to the closet to hang up her coat and at once found balm from the little wrinkled pomander ball swinging between her clothes.

Sunsoaked walls, bee-loud days, all summer in your hand. She stood breathing it, and remembering back. Then she gave a little start of surprise, for she was not remembering back at all, she was thinking forward, and they were thoughts she had never thought before.

She closed the closet door and went to bed.

CHAPTER FOUR

THE next morning, the morning of the Hoon Hay fête, came soft and caressing. It gave an early promise to grow to one of those calm days when the blue of the sky seems to soak itself into the earth. What would happen when it soaked into mountains already blue simply took the breath away. Libby, reluctantly prising herself from the window to which she had leapt as soon as she had wakened to see what the weather had bestowed, shivered in anticipation. She ran to shower, not noticing that she was humming a satisfied little song.

But when she went to dress, the satisfaction dimmed. Really, Pam might have packed something other than that blue number. It was not that she didn't like it, she loved it, but blue on a day like this, in a place like this, was just too much. She rifled the closet again and again, refusing to be soothed by the nostalgic airs of the swinging pomander ball, but found that unless she wore a too-warm winter weight, and one couldn't, or an office-y blouse and skirt, and one shouldn't, it would have to be the blue linen. Such a *blue* blue, too. No undertones or subtleties. Blue.

She went in to waken Barbary, but the little girl was already flattening her nose at the window also to check the day. So the excitement had reached her, too. It was no trouble this morning to bath her. The sooner the washing was done, Barbary's mind was undoubtedly ticking, the sooner they could go up the hill to the big castle-house again, to Friendly, the black dog, and to those promised cornets of fairy floss.

Libby took the opportunity of the girl's amiability to break the news about the other little girls who were to join her here at Clove Orange. She had no illusions about Barbary. Although, child-like, in her heart she really would welcome companions of her own age and sex, the mature woman in every young female also would protest against being no longer the sole female. For, of course, old people like Mrs. Dawson and Libby simply did not count.

Barbary, however, evinced little interest, except to say : "One—I hope it isn't Gloria, Two : If it's Susan I'm going to bite her !"

The only interest, apart from the contemplated fairy floss, that she did show was in the colour of her dress. Libby had taken out a rosy pink. Barbary looked at it with clear refusal in her eyes and intoned instead, "Blue."

"No, darling, pink."

"Blue."

"Everything's going to be blue today, if you are, too, you could get lost in all that blueness. I mean, Barbary, too much is—well, too much."

"Blue," Barbary repeated.

"Barbary !" Libby said sternly, steeling her heart against the little stuck-out bottom lip. She could remember setting her heart on colours in just the same way when she was a child, and had she not been wearing, through necessity, this blue that she did, she would have given in at once. But, sensitively, she could imagine Pierce Hardway's quick look at the two of them, then the lifted brow. Probably a supercilious lift. So : "No," she said.

What would have happened then, Libby well knew. Barbary would have thrown a tantrum that would be more ear-catching even than the blue dress was eye-catching, and Mr. Clove Orange, coming to investigate, would still have raised the supercilious brow, this time at Libby's lack of child management. But, passing by at that moment, Pierce Hardway heard Barbary's urgent "Blue," and put his head round the door and concurred cheerfully, "That's right, blue dresses for our girls, blue ties for our boys. Good morning, Miss Meadows." The eyes went briefly up and down Libby, undoubtedly censoriously as she had thought, and buttoning Barbary into the blue, now that he had ordered it, Libby waited to be chided for depriving a small girl.

But as Barbary ran out excitedly, Pierce apologized, "Sorry for butting in, but I could hear how the youngster felt. I expect to her it's a blue day."

"Well, I didn't put this on because of the day." Libby was snappy. "I put it on because it's the only suitable dress Pam packed."

"And blue. I should know that, seeing I particularly instructed Pam."

"You did *what*?" she gasped.

"I knew you would be coming to the fête, so—"

"How could you know? I was to have been back in Sydney by now."

"I knew you would be coming," he said, ignoring her interruption, "and I could see you at it in just this colour."

There was no answer to that, no answer, anyway, that one could fling without being personal. One could scarcely say, "How does it come about that you even remotely think of me, let alone see me in a certain colour?"

A little at a loss, Libby mumbled her reason for depriving Barbary : the superfluity of blue.

"Never blue," he refused. Before she could argue, he said, "Quick breakfast this morning, Mrs. Dawson has been prevailed upon to put it down to tea and toast."

"A good thing," agreed Libby, "for probably the boys will be downing hamburgers and popcorn all day."

"And you will be downing dishes of strawberries?" He was looking at her with the brows raised now in the supercilious manner she had anticipated for the two blue dresses.

"One, anyway." Her tone was challenging. If she had expected a dish from Pierce Hardway she was disappointed.

Going down the passage by his side Libby asked, "Do the boys attending school go to the Hoon Hay fête, too?"

"No school today. No school in all the mountains. Indeed, not many shops will be open this afternoon. It's quite a function."

"To benefit—?"

"This answer will please you. Among other charities, mostly local, the B.W.C."

That did please Libby and she admitted it.

"Though I expect," she added, "it was an obligatory inclusion."

"Obligatory?" He looked puzzled. "Oh, you would mean my friendship with the Abbersons ... with Tessa."

"No." She felt annoyed at his interpretation. "I referred to all the voluntary things you've probably done to help the fête along."

"You're quite right of course. Apart from assisting with the erection of the stalls, etcetera, we run a contributing stall ourselves."

"Herbs?"

"What else?" he smiled. "Most fête-goers are women, and from women you can always depend on a sale of lovage or lad's love."

"Wormwood?"

"I see," he said blandly, opening the dining-room door, "you have been studying my herbs."

Cups were set out and the huge teapot was working overtime. Pierce poured for Libby and brought her a slice of toast spread with honey of roses.

"Cut the white heels from red roses," she remembered, biting appreciatively. "What came next?"

"Add the pressed-off liquid to honey," he told her, "afterwards boil and bottle. Like it?"

"Ambrosia!" she smiled.

"A pity you're not better up in the herbs, we could have you on the counter today, answering the questions."

"I can still sell," she offered.

"You will be, don't worry. If not with us, then certainly with someone else. No doubt Tessa will have her eye on you for the honesty stall."

"Honesty?"

"Lunaria. It grows well up here."

"Oh, the silvery, wafery flower that looks artificial but isn't."

"That is its dried and peeled form, actually the blossom is blue." He smiled teasingly at Libby. "We can't get away from blue, can we?"

"What is done with the honesty?" she asked.

"It's sold in bunches. It goes well, I'm told. Have you honesty fingers?" He had taken up her hand, but in such a matter-of-fact way that it did not draw one glance from any of the boys, nor from Mrs. Dawson. For such a matter-of-fact gesture, Libby was annoyed that her heart beat so rapidly, that the fingers that held hers felt so warm that the warmth seemed to reach farther than finger-deep.

The meal over, the boys lined up, and Pierce Hardway passed down their ranks to make sure that shoes were cleaned, ties knotted and hair brushed. Barbary had lined up with them, and on an impulse Libby went and lined up beside her.

When Pierce came to Barbary he said, "Let me see, madam, isn't that a smudge there?" and he touched one of the ticklish spots. Barbary immediately doubled up with mirth. But when he reached Libby there was no laughter in the long look he levelled at her, a rather strange look, almost—if looks could be that—a reaching one. Oddly disconcerted, not feeling funny any more, Libby dropped out of the rank.

"Inspection satisfactory," called Pierce Hardway. "See to it that your behaviour today is the same. All right, boys, disperse." He put a detaining hand on both Libby and Barbary as they also went to move, and asked, "Since when have you two changed sex?"

"I'm seven, not six," protested Barbary, and Libby

explained, "I just thought you meant all the assembly. Don't we walk up with the rest?"

"You, Mrs. Dawson and Barbary ride up with me. And not in the ute or the Holden, but in my Sunday best car. You haven't seen that yet—it's my pride and joy, I bought it to mark a recent climb up the ladder. The monetary ladder I refer to. I would culebrate in a different way if it was another sort of success. Meanwhile, we couldn't arrive in anything less than Black Beauty, as I named it, not down that red carpet."

"Will there be a red carpet?" asked Barbary, wide-eyed. "A red carpet for a motor car?"

"No, but there's a fine red gravel drive, a very beautiful drive, and on either side of the drive there will be important people, several brass bands, all the trimmings."

"It sounds," said Libby, taking Barbary's hand and following Pierce Hardway, "quite an important event."

"There are several such events annually in the Blue Mountains. The Rhododendron Festival, the Week of the Leaves. And then other private gardens are opened, as today with Hoon Hay." They had reached the garages ... there were several of them, in one was the B.W.C. Mini ... and out of the largest Pierce backed a large car. Not the ute as he had said, nor the Holden, but something much more affluent. Barbary squealed with pleasure at the sight of it, and Libby in spite of herself could not help feeling impressed. Mrs. Dawson panted up in her best navy blue and Pierce bowed them in.

Mrs. Dawson got in the back, and Barbary, eyeing the stately roominess there, followed her. "Now I'm the Queen!" she thrilled.

It was a luxury car with ample space for more even than three in the one seat, but Pierce shut the door definitely and indicated for Libby to sit beside him. He went round to the driver's seat, and smoothly they moved off, Barbary, carried away with the grandeur, bowing graciously from side to side.

Libby smiled at the little hand acknowledging the encroaching gums and ti-tree of the bush road. "She really thinks she is," she murmured.

"And why not? It's the prerogative of all females. Aren't *you* someone's princess?"

She was silent, achingly silent, for like all daughters, she had been her father's. She did not realize that her quiet answered him so clearly until he drawled, "So you are, Miss Meadows."

She did not correct, "No, but I was," and he drawled again, "Can one ask whose?"

"No." Her reply was unadorned, and any further comment he might have made was drowned in the blare of a brass band and in Barbary's shrill of joy at the booming drums. With a regal swing to suit the small princess ... *two* princesses? asked Pierce Hardway's quizzically lifted brow ... they turned into the wide drive of Hoon Hay.

Libby had thought that the elegance she had sensed from her first distant scrutiny of the mountain house would have prepared her for the elegance at nearer quarters, but in that instant of entry she knew she was totally unprepared for the distinction, the dignity, the charm. She drew in her breath at hand-hewn stone parapets contrasting with the pink timber, at fluted pillars, at twin staircases curving exquisitely to meet each other in a complicated and delicate design. She saw lovely flagged verandahs, courts, benches, sundials, fountains, rock-scalloped pools where lily pads dipped and gold carp played.

Behind these she saw gardened acres, the mountain climate flowers unfolding their colours and tendernesses to emerald plush lawns, mingling their sweet blossom airs with the minty tanging of piney earth and evergreen shrubs. She gave a little shiver of joy.

"Takes your breath away, doesn't it?" said Pierce by Libby's side.

"Yes," was all Libby could breathe.

Barbary was silenced for a while, too, but the enchantment of the little striped fête tents now appearing for them on the largest square of all of emerald plush lawn unloosened her tongue again and she chorused her approval in many ecstatic oohs and ahs.

Mrs. Dawson, past breathless impacts by now, was busy unwrapping a capacious apron.

"Looks like good business," she said, satisfied. "Put me off here, Pierce. I won't wait for you to park the car, the boys might need a hand."

"But would they be here yet?" inquired Libby.

"Some of them went quite early this morning to get the stall ready," Pierce informed her, stopping the car and leaning over to open the door for Mrs. Dawson, "and even the rest would beat us up here. It's only half a hill, as you discovered yesterday, if you take the back track from Clove Orange."

Mrs. Dawson was getting out and Barbary was scrambling after her. Libby opened her door.

"The child will be all right," advised Pierce. "There are plenty of watching eyes here. Usually there are even eyes from B.W.C. I mean V.I.P. eyes, not the blue eyes of cadets." As she did not comment, he resumed, "Mr. Perkins always attended. However, this year, a member being on tap, he has evidently left the representation to you."

"There seem to be representatives of many bodies," said Libby, taking in the thronging crowds.

"They come by car and train from Sydney, suburbs and country. Last Hoon Hay fête there were even interstaters. I see you are getting out, too."

"I thought I might be able to help as well as Mrs. Dawson on the Clove Orange stall."

"She could sell the herbal cosmetics," nodded Mrs. Dawson. "The boys hate that and I've scarcely the right complexion."

"You've a genuine honeysuckle and sage look about you, Dawsie," complimented Pierce.

"Basil vinegar and nettle, more like it," said Mrs. Dawson resignedly. "There's your honeysuckle young man." She smiled at Libby.

"Blue-starred borage," corrected Pierce. Tessa, too, had said that. Turning to Barbary he said, "No, not porridge, Miss Smarty, borage, so wipe that smile off your face."

"I wasn't so smiling!" Barbary started to protest indignantly, then began giggling. If it had been meant as a compliment, it ended in laughter, for which Libby was rather relieved.

She followed behind Mrs. Dawson to the Clove Orange stall.

The herb phials and packets were set out very attractively, and already the boys were doing a fine trade.

"You won't need an apron," directed Mrs. Dawson. "Telling customers whether they should use rosemary, geranium or lavender lotions doesn't require a kitchen look like when I tell them how to bake fish with marjoram leaves."

She was doing just that the next minute, her rosy round face looking as though she had just come from the stove, and certainly not looking, thought Libby, vastly relieved, as it had looked a few days ago when she had been laid low with her migraine.

Libby sold sachets of dried orange blossom for face packs and ounces of dried wallflowers for water-softening. Lavender bags were much in demand, and rosemary rubbing lotions. She found it all great fun, and was reluctant to go when Mrs. Dawson told her it was time she did the rounds of the fête.

"We're all rostered," explained Mrs. Dawson. "Pierce is very emphatic over that, he says we all must have our turn away from the stall. I'm off to the tea tent. Will you come?"

"After I look round." For the first time since she stepped behind the Clove Orange display and got straight into action, Libby looked round now. "But Mr

Hardway isn't here," she said, surprised, for she had thought that naturally he would be working on his own counter.

"Oh, no, he's always claimed by the V.I.P.s," said Mrs. Dawson, and Libby could well believe that. In spite of her absorption on her arrival she had still noticed the bows and acknowledgments afforded to the herb baron. Almost red carpet esteem.

She slipped under the bench and strolled out to the green lawn. Barbary had disappeared, but she did not take much pinpointing; she was underneath the biggest and rosiest fairy floss cornet on the entire ground, which meant that Peter Abberson—

"Her second," said a voice in Libby's ear. "Are you going to scold me? I am assured it's only spun sugar blown up to gigantic quantities."

It was Peter himself, the face she had thought so likeable yesterday even more likeable at a second meeting. Libby smiled back at the young man and assured him, "No."

"Strawberries?" he asked. "Or after all that trade would you prefer tea?"

"Can I have both? I mean the tea first and then the strawberries?"

"You're a girl after my own heart!" He was leading her to the tea tent.

There was an official table in the tent and the V.I.P.s were taking their tea there. But Pierce was not among them. Neither was Tessa Abberson... not that Libby had expected her to be after her sarcastic outcries.

The tea came, and the usual array of home-made cakes and scones.

"Leave room for the strawberries," smiled Peter.

He was quite charming, and exceedingly relaxing and amusing to talk to. Only when Tessa's name entered the conversation did his smooth equanimity lose some of its easy pleasantry, although, Libby thought, she might only be imagining that faint pause, that brief hesitation.

"Where is Tessa?" she asked directly at last.

"With Pierce. Of course."

It did not answer the question because Libby did not know where Pierce was, but evidently where he was, Tessa was, too. Of course.

She got up, rather abruptly. The light fête chair fell back and had to be replaced.

"You haven't had a second cup and you've left the cakes," Peter reproached.

"The strawberries," she reminded him, "room for," and escaped to the green plush lawn again. Of course, she was thinking. Of course!

She was so exasperated with herself that it was all she could do not to race down the hill, climb the fence that divided Hoon Hay from Clove Orange and run home.

Run home. *Home*, she had said. More exasperated with herself than ever, Libby began a determined round of the fair. As though it mattered one iota if Tessa was with—

She patronized the Aunt Sally, the Fish Pond, the Lucky Envelope Stall, bought a basket of French jellies from the Sweets and a tatted handkerchief from the Handicraft. She stood and listened to a band rendition and guessed the number of peas in a bottle. As fairs went, she decided, slowly calmly down again, the Hoon Hay fête was a very pleasant one.

By now she had reached the striped tent that evidently housed the fair's fortune-teller. Its entrance was appropriately hung with the right sort of cryptic-looking curtains, material you could faintly and mysteriously see through but not see clearly enough to be mundanely disillusioned. The drapes made the small interior interestingly dark, rendered the veiled handmaiden waiting on the sage, soothsayer, whatever he was, very intriguing. Libby consulted the sign above the tent and saw that instead of the usual palmistry or tea-leaf reading, here your fate was determined through sand-divining. Well, she had patronized everything else, she smiled, opening her purse.

The veiled handmaiden bowed her in, waved her to sit beside a sand tray. Then the handmaiden clanged a cymbal for the diviner to attend.

In the greenish gloom the figures were barely discernible, so Libby stopped blinking into the dark in an effort to see what her attendants looked like, and instead traced her index finger through the sand, as the handmaiden silently demonstrated, then waited to hear her fate from the diviner, who had quietly entered and knelt down beside her; all foolish, of course, but fun.

And at first when the diviner spoke, it remained fun. He said in a deep, muffled voice, probably deep by design, and muffled because he spoke behind the folds of a draped sheet : "Certain affairs are about to take place that will alter your career. You will travel to strange places, meet new people." Libby had to clench tight her teeth not to conclude for the oracle : "You will take a long journey that will end in lots of joy," for she, too, had been a soothsayer in a fête, and had learned her patter, no doubt, from the same book.

Then abruptly it was not just fun, and most certainly it was not from a book.

For Pierce Hardway, abruptly discarding the deep tone, the loosened folds of the sheet revealing the strong lines of his lean face at the same time as they unmuffled the next words he spoke, was not reciting from the book. From any book.

He said almost as though it was said for him : "The sands of time are written, and this is what they say : You will not travel to strange places, you will come home."

Home! That was what she had thought in her exasperation when she had come from the tea-tent; she had thought : "I will run home."

But home was—was— Well, home wasn't really anywhere now, it was just the latest bedsitter. Where it would be in the future, only her salary and the current room availability could tell, but one thing it would not, could not, be where she instinctively had turned in her curious unease after talking **with** Peter, it would not, could not be Clove Orange.

"Really, Pierce!" Tessa's voice broke through the odd silence that held them both, held Libby and Hardway, broke through the greenish gloom.

"Really, Pierce, that's more than Miss Meadows paid for."

"So it is." Pierce Hardway was smiling through the folds now, and the smile was very white against his brown skin, a skin even darker in the dim light. "Perhaps Miss Meadows would care to pay an extra fee," he suggested.

"I've patronized every stall," Libby informed him, "and my purse is growing light."

"That is the goal," said Tessa, coming forward, pushing aside her handmaiden veils and taking out a cigarette. "The idea, the Julius idea, is not simply to let the purse grow light but to deplete the purse."

"Fair enough," decided Libby, "when it's to benefit B.W.C."

"That's dog-in-the-manger," reproved Pierce casually. "Why not fair enough for any of the Hoon Hay causes?"

"Most of all," put in Tessa stringently, "the cause of the patron himself."

"But he doesn't benefit," protested Libby.

"Not monetarily, but—ah, there are other rewards." At Libby's confused look, she intoned, "The moment of entry, the hushed deference, the brass fanfare, the ringing applause."

"You mean Uncle Julius—Mr. Abberson has not made an appearance yet?"

Tessa did not deign to answer that, she merely flung Libby a look of scorn.

"Then the pulling of forelocks," she went on, "the dropped curtsies."

Pierce interrupted quite severely, "Enough of those exaggerations, Tessa, you're being absurd."

"Am I?" Tessa held up a hand for silence, and through the tent walls emanated the definite stir of something happening, an excitement, a ripple, a flux of anticipation. Then almost at once the brass bands struck up: "The hills of home."

"There was a soldier, a Scottish soldier—"

"It's *his* theme," disparaged Tessa, "he, who is neither Scottish nor militant, except militant in his treatment of others."

"Tessa!" Pierce's sharp voice succeeded in stemming, if only temporarily, Tessa's derision. "You are as aware as I am that Julius Abberson is of Scot descent and that his army record—"

Tessa tilted her chin, but evidently could think of no immediate retort.

The brief theme was finishing, at the last note of the trumpet the applause broke out. More magnetised than curious, though she was unaware of the magnetism, Libby moved to the flap of the tent.

There was no forelock-pulling, of course, and no curtsies, but as the tall, thin, silver-haired figure came slowly down the gracious stone stairs from the big pink house, from the ranks on each side of him rippled the same profound deference that could have been coupled with all of Tessa's exaggerations. Why, Libby thought, I almost bobbed myself.

"You see!" Tessa was by Libby's side now, reading her reaction, gauging it, and her voice was terse.

"Mr. Abberson. Uncle Julius," she said.

CHAPTER FIVE

OF all the reactions that Libby had expected upon her first encounter with Julius Abberson, and there was no denying that because of that faint air of encircling mystery she *had* thought about him, the reaction she did experience now took her by surprise. It was neither like, dislike, sympathy or aversion, in fact any stimulus at all—save a sense of familiarity. *Somewhere she had seen Uncle Julius before.*

Her memory, examined, told her she had not, her common sense backed that up, but still the feeling persisted. Somewhere I have seen him, or someone like him. I know I have.

She thought back to her own grandfather, not far removed from the same vintage, had he been alive, as that silver-haired patriarch now descending the beautiful column of stairs, doing it with a nobility that had to be witnessed to be believed. She watched Julius Abberson pause to speak to a small boy, touching his head as he did so, she watched him pat the hair of a small girl, shake hands with a man, bow graciously to a woman. All done with a glorious patronage and a shining charm she had never known before. And yet—and yet she had seen him.

Not Uncle Julius perhaps, but the fellow image that now eluded her. Never Grandfather in New Zealand, in spite of a near vintage, of a likeness in build, for Grandy had not been that aristocratic type. More—well, chicory and coriander. She smiled at her metaphor. A week ago, before she had come to Clove Orange, she would never have thought in such terms. But for this man, for Julius Abberson, she could find no descriptive herb. In short, smiling again to herself, he wasn't. Not J.A.

"Failing being king or emperor or some other cock of

the walk he would have liked to have been the head of a tremendous family," Tessa was intoning drily at Libby's side. "You know, one of those people who put on a vast annual family reunion, and it's attended by his twelve children, his twelve twelve times grandchildren, twelve twelve twelve times—"

"No family at all?" interrupted Libby. "Yet you told me you had legions of uncles and aunts."

"I meant Peter," Tessa said sharply. "Yes, there are legions. But all very distant Abbersons. Offshoots, really. But because it pleases him to do so, each one is graciously if patronizingly accepted. It has to be them or no one, you see, for J.A. never married."

"You would think he would have liked to have married, have founded a family of his own," proffered Libby, "that is if what you tell of him is true."

"It's true. But a personal family would have been a drawback. I mean one's own child would ask something of one, wouldn't it? Something more than a gentle nod and a kingly pat."

"Tessa, you should be labelled poison," said Pierce rather mildly for such a strong statement. His interest was more on Libby, he was watching Libby watching Uncle Julius. His eyes were narrowed.

"Bells ringing," he insinuated softly, so softly that only Libby heard. She understood at once that he had read her sense of recognition, and she looked at him in question.

"I, too," he said still softly, "have felt I've met him before."

Tessa had moved back into the tent where she was removing her handmaiden veils, so there was no fear of her hearing.

"Where?" asked Libby.

Pierce did not reply, but his eyes flicked.

While Libby watched in fascination the almost regal procession of Julius Abberson through the ranks of the people, Pierce questioned Tessa about her veil removal.

"We've finished," she said definitely. "Libby was our last customer. If you don't believe me, look at the kitty. Much more takings than last year."

"Your Uncle Julius might patronize the sand-diviners."

"He won't. He'd be afraid of what he might hear."

"Not from me, Tessa."

"No, not from you, nor anybody else, it seems. Every-one kow-tows."

For such a bitter statement, Pierce's response was still mild. He simply shook his head at her, then gently patted the red head.

"Leave me alone!" Tessa burst out quite violently.

"How can I, my dear," he said smoothly, "if I'm to be to you what you plan?" His smile teased her.

But she could not regain her equanimity that quickly. "Just—just don't pat me," she said. "He does that. Just —just don't." She had finished her handmaiden removal and was combing her lovely red hair. "Come on, Libby." It was more a command than an invitation. "Come and meet the top brass."

Julius Abberson was graciously disengaging himself from another of the many groups pushing forward eagerly to meet him. Libby watched him intrigued. Even from here she could see he had that art of looking on a parcel of people as though he was looking at each individually. She could see by the sparkling faces that each of them took that look as for them alone.

By her side Tessa confirmed Libby's thoughts. "They believe he recognizes them, but if they only knew." She gave a low laugh. "J.A. only sees himself."

"And you and Peter," included Libby.

"We are, or are intended to be, himself."

The band was concluding another rendition, it was a Scottish medley, and Tessa pointed out testily that it again included the Abberson signature tune. "Look," she indicated to Libby, "the Vicar is going to make the

customary complimentary noises now, complimentary to
J.A."

"Well, after all it is his house that has been opened,"
protested Libby fairly.

"And doesn't he bask in that!" Tessa came back.

The speeches, as the irreverent Tessa had said, were
extremely flattering, but accepted as they were in complete and charming humility by Uncle Julius, the praise
more glowed around him than accosted the ears, it made
a halo of words for the shining silver head. "Why, he's
sweet!" Libby said impulsively.

Tessa smiled thinly.

Then Uncle Julius was responding, and his voice was
warm and rich. He said the expected things ... how
happy was Hoon Hay to open its doors again ... how
honoured, how very honoured his family ...

"His family," echoed Tessa. All at once she tugged
on Libby's arm. "Come on, I can't stand any more."

"But I want to meet him." Libby, watching the gracious contact of man and group felt she, too, must anticipate.

"Don't worry, you'll be meeting him, even if you tried
to avoid him you'd still find yourself face to face. J.A.'s
no fool, he knows what's going on."

"What do you mean?"

"You, Peter, me, Pierce."

"But it isn't."

"It is," said Tessa brazenly, "so far as I'm concerned."

"Well, you know your own business, Tessa, but so far
as I'm concerned I'm not in any of this."

Tessa broke in with her characteristic directness.
"What's wrong with Peter?"

"Nothing, of course. He's charming. But—"

Tessa interrupted forcefully again, "That's enough,
then. It's sufficient basis."

"It isn't, though. I'd want—well, I'd want more."

"Like?"

"Like—love," Libby said diffidently.

"Love!" Tessa's laugh was derisive. "You're a nice litle fuddy-duddy," she awarded Libby, "but you've been reading too much romantic fiction, either that or breathing Mrs. Dawson's lavender bags."

"No," Libby said a little abstractedly. "Pomander balls."

They had reached the honesty stall by now, where the bunches of peeled honesty ... lunaria ... had already all been sold. Pierce had said they made a quick return. Seeing Libby's interested eyes on some remnant bunches of the dry flowers, Tessa showed her how to peel them to the thin, fairy spheres that were so popular to tide over budless periods, and Libby, with her smaller, slimmer fingers, soon learned the knack.

It was while she rubbed her thumb and forefinger together, removing skin after skin until the fairy shape emerged, that Uncle Julius came up at last. He went first to Tessa, and Libby watched while the girl stood quite still under his gentle pat, and then his greeting kiss, the old dry lips touching the young blooming brow. She was keenly aware of a tenseness in Tessa, of a strain nearing breaking point, and she thought with sudden clarity: "This silver honesty in my hands is the real Tessa, frail, delicate, sensitive, and not the husk of hardness like the husk I've just peeled away."

She watched the old man's tender bestowal of the kiss, acutely aware of a brief moment of defences down in the girl, so brief it was barely a moment at all. And then Libby was watching something else, something she found almost unbelievable: a sense of supplication, she could almost call it entreaty, in Julius Abberson. But why, Libby wondered, would the king of a castle entreat? Bestow, yes, but *entreat*? Uncle Julius?

The little tableau fascinated her. She stood plucking absently at the petals as she watched, conscious even more than before of that pre-knowledge of Julius Abberson, and to that pose of girl and silver petal the old man turned from his foster-niece to Libby, bowing in his inimitable way, at the same time taking her hands in his.

"Good honesty hands," he awarded graciously, "more slender and sensitive than yours, Tessa my darling. However, I would prefer one pretty hand to hold the flowers so that I could kiss the other hand. Ah, that's better." For Libby, with almost immature eagerness, had put the stems in the one hand and quite anxiously extended the other. "Greetings, my dear," said Julius Abberson. "Tessa child, you haven't yet presented this delightful young woman."

Libby felt the dry lips on her hand at the same time as she heard Tessa's flat, "She's Libby Meadows, from Clove Orange."

"So," Julius Abberson said.

He stood regarding Libby quite pleasantly but—and Libby, for all her fascination, could not doubt this—*shrewdly.*

"You must bring Miss Meadows—may an old man use Libby, most charming, most attractive, my dear ... to our Afters, Tessa child."

"I don't think she'd care to come." Tessa, quite recovered now, was her old rude self again.

Evidently Uncle Julius understood her moods. His beautiful brows raised very slightly, his beautiful mouth quirked gently, as he said, "I think you could be mistaken, my dear."

And of course Tessa was mistaken. Wild horses would not now have kept Libby from the Abberson Afters, whatever that was.

Tessa explained astringently as the tall, gracious figure took his courtly adieux and moved to his next audience.

"It's a Thing that happens every year after the visitors have gone away. All the family, and any others that it pleases Uncle Julius to include, take sherry and biscuits in the big drawing room and watch the king hold audience." She yawned.

"Tessa, why are you like this?" Libby could not help a remonstration. "Nothing missed me just now. You were as tense as a bird, but"—Libby paused—"you were also eager."

"I'll give you in the tenseness. That man unnerves me. But the eagerness, oh, no. Next you'll accuse me of liking Uncle Julius."

"No," said Libby slowly, thoughtfully, "but I might use—love."

"Love? Love *him*?" Tessa's voice was sharp. "You must be crazed."

"All right," placated Libby, who even in this short a time had realized that the only way to handle the girl was to retreat whenever a storm threatened. "No love, not even any liking. That brings me to my invitation. Why am I asked?"

"Some people are, people Uncle Julius takes a fancy to, I just told you. Probably he sees an honesty-peeling future in you and wants to keep you on his side."

"Don't be foolish."

"All right then, I'll tell you the real reason. He wants you there because, being J.A., he has undoubtedly already heard what the grapevine is whispering."

"What's that?" asked Libby.

"In a Blue Mountains town with only the Three Sisters Rocks or the Orphan Rock to gossip about, why, you and Pierce, of course."

"Don't be foolish." Again Libby said it.

"Oh, you and I know it's foolish." Tessa's eyes narrowed remindingly, reminding Libby of her own intention to marry Pierce. "But to J.A. it would be very pleasant news."

"Why?"

"Because it would scotch that other news. Pierce and *Tessa*. Now do you see?"

"But would Uncle Julius really know about any of it? He's so—well, so ivory tower."

"His tower has windows." Again the bitter note. "It has a spy-glass, too."

"Tessa!"

"Now you sound like Pierce." Tessa's voice was weary. "Look, you know you really want to come, so don't quibble about it. Just accept the honoured invitation to the Abberson Afters in the right deferential spirit, then ask your questions when it's over, not before. Only"—Tessa was closing up the stall, and Libby saw that stalls were being closed all around her now, realized that it was getting late—"don't ask me."

By the first half light of evening and the first prick of an early star, all the canvas was removed. It spoke well for the Abberson rule that an army of helpers had come forward and removed each paper wrapper, every shred of litter. In the pale larkspur light of a Blue Mountains evening Libby saw the beautiful lawns and shrubberies emerge as they were intended, space, leafage, blossom and fragrance instead of striped awning.

"I must say in all fairness that J.A. is an organizer," admitted Tessa grudgingly. "Most houses opened up like Hoon Hay take days to recover, but not the Abberson domicile. Come on." She turned to Libby. "We now take ourselves inside."

Libby followed Tessa up one of the twin stairways, pausing at the exquisite curved meeting of the two flights to turn back and drink in the beauty of the mountain home.

Tessa had paused with her, and when Libby asked, "Is it very old?" she replied, "Old for Australia. It followed soon after the mountain-crossing explorers, if you know our history dates."

"Have there been Abbersons ever since?"

"All Abbersons. I often wonder if those other A's were like Julius. When I look around me I think, 'No.' To achieve beauty like this one would have had to have a soul, and J.A.—" She shrugged. "However, he's the sole descendant. All the cousins, uncles and aunts you will see assembled now are faraways. Even Peter. Though"—tightly—"he is still an *A*."

She took Libby's arm. "Come into the parlour, though anything less like a parlour you'll never see."

Libby walked behind Tessa into a vast vestibule. After the grounds of Hoon Hay she had expected a certain elegance and beauty, but not the grandeur that at once confronted her. It all started with the crimson carpet with the fleur de lys design, with the silk wall panels, with the corded bell-pulls. Then there was the subtle opening by folding doors into room after room, the impact of each room more arresting than its predecessor, the decor so regally lovely that it left Libby gasping, so that by the time she finally reached the big drawing room with its glittering chandelier and its air of almost enthronement she was breathless.

Uncle Julius sat in the middle of the room, and though the large chair in which he rested was floor level, he seemed somehow to be on a dais . . . or was that the effect of his gracious person sitting perfectly straight yet still serenely relaxed, with the shining silver head slightly to one side as he regarded his "children" with a gentle, quizzical smile?

Sherry was being brought round, plates of Abernethy biscuits. "It's always Abernethy," whispered Tessa. "It's like the signature tune, an Abberson Thing."

"Don't spoil it," entreated Libby, entranced.

Tessa looked at her derisively. "You, too?"

The cousins, uncles, aunts—offshoots, as Tessa had described them—were fussing round the centre chair. So was the Vicar, evidently another chosen guest. Had Pierce Hardway been included? Libby glanced around and saw the height of the herb baron above the rest, even above Peter Abberson who was very tall himself.

"He's going to speak," said Tessa. Her hand was on Libby's. Libby saw that it shook.

Julius Abberson had the silver touch in his speech as well as his looks. It was a pleasure to listent to him.

He charmingly included all the non-A's present in his warm greeting, looking around in that way of his that made each one think he was personally greeting them. Libby, anyway, felt he smiled warmly and personally at her.

Then he greeted his kin, performing the same gracious personal image.

"And," he said finally, lovingly and very clearly, "Tessa."

Tessa lowered her head.

He spoke of his pleasure in the annual fêtes, how the family reunion meant as much to him as his very life-blood. When he got to the "very", Tessa finished for him in a small voice, "life-blood."

She looked sidelong at Libby. "I know the build-ups off by heart," she told her softly. "I should do, I've heard them all my life. It's what comes after that I don't know. That's the trap he springs. Once when I was a schoolgirl it was me. Some heinous childish sin. Once it was Uncle Claud . . . that's him in the brown suit . . . he had annoyed J.A. and he got it in the neck at one of these Afters. Not by name, of course, Uncle Julius doesn't need to trot out names, he keeps his sheep in order with a silvery word."

"Hush, Tessa!" whispered Libby anxiously.

"You bet I will, I want to hear whose flesh is to be burned now."

Libby touched her hand warningly, for Uncle Julius had paused, and there was in that pause an almost pregnant preparation for what was to come.

Fluently, even lightly, it did come, so lightly and seemingly unintentionally that it was some time before Libby realized what Julius Abberson was saying. No, not actually saying, but inclining, rimming around.

She knew that Tessa had grown rigid by her side, that the rest of them personally concerned, Peter, Pierce, herself, were just as rigid. For that was the art of Uncle Julius. The silvery tongue that so fascinated also subtly commanded.

As in a trance Libby listened, sipped her sherry, nibbled her Abernethy.

Then, some time later, presenting her hand to be kissed by Julius Abberson again, she took her leave.

Getting into the car with Pierce, she said factually, "What happened to the others?"

"Someone would drive Mrs. Dawson and Barbary back, and the boys would foot it again." He was being just as factual back.

He swung the big car out of the red gravel drive, but this time there was no Barbary to bow to the bordering eucalypts . . . though it should have been, Libby knew now, to Uncle Julius.

"Was it all true?" she asked unreally. "Up there?"

Pierce was garaging the car by now; it had been a completely silent journey.

"Presumably you heard as well as I did," he answered.

"Why didn't anyone interrupt?"

"Perhaps they were hypnotised," he suggested. "I've often suspected J.A. of having that power."

"It was unbelievable. I mean for a man to say in that silky voice all that he did, for a man to order . . . oh, yes, it was an order, for all that gentleness . . . as he did, yet not one person to intervene."

"There were only four really interested," Pierce reminded her rather lazily. "The rest just looked on."

"But surely out of that four—You, for instance," Libby said angrily. "You're not the type to be hypnotised by silky talk."

"No, I wasn't hypnotised."

"Then—?"

"Perhaps," said Pierce still lazily, "I didn't disagree with what J.A. decreed."

At her startled look he elaborated, "That all this misdirected dalliance between four people must cease—oh, not in such direct words, of course, but certainly that was the trend and the message, wasn't it?"

"Yes," breathed Libby, still incredulous, "he, Julius Abberson, quite brazenly—"

"No, never brazenly, Libby, not J.A."

Libby ignored him. "He not only directed Peter to Tessa, which was to be expected in a way, but he—he—"

"He paired you and me," put in Pierce, still lazily. "More than that, he even married us off. And he did it all so subtly, he never really actually said it in one single word. You know"—thoughtfully—"you have to admire that old boy."

"But it was unspeakable," broke in Libby furiously. "I mean perhaps it's all right for him to settle Peter and Tessa, but—"

"My child, to settle their affair he had to settle ours as well. He's no fool, old J.A., he knows the way the breeze is blowing, Tessa's futile little breeze."

"Futile?" she queried.

"As far as I'm concerned," said Pierce.

Anger and incredulity still held Libby in its grip. "And you stood by and let him say those things," she repeated. "Were you afraid to interrupt?"

"Afraid?" Pierce laughed. "No. But I was entertained."

"Entertained? But, it was quite dreadful to be announced like that."

"Yes," agreed Pierce, "almost like calling the banns, wasn't it?" He laughed again.

"Don't take it so lightly," stormed Libby; she was shaken by that performance in Hoon Hay.

"How else?" Pierce Hardway flicked back. "Take it seriously? Like this?" Leaning over, he deliberately took Libby into his arms. "The kiss of betrothal?" he taunted, putting his lips on hers.

The travesty of it enraged her, and yet, she thought, seriousness was the last thing she wanted; he was quite right in this mock attitude. But she was annoyed with the difficulty that she, a fellow actor in the farce, found in withdrawing herself.

"It was all unbelievable," she repeated rather wildly. "When Tessa told me yesterday how he ruled, I thought she was exaggerating. But it's true. *True*. Yet he can't direct two lives like that."

"Four." Pierce was lighting up his pipe.

"I'm not counting us," she said impatiently.

"J.A. was."

"Only to rid Tessa and Peter of obstacles," reminded Libby. She began again, "How dare a man demand that that pair—"

"He didn't," Pierce reminded her. "Not in actual words."

"And yet," said Libby, "a demand was there." She turned to Pierce in wonder. "Why? Why?"

"He wants the line continued, the Abberson line."

"It could be with a girl of Peter's own choice."

"Perhaps Tessa is Peter's choice. I don't know Peter Abberson very well, but I shouldn't imagine he's as malleable as all that." He was closing the garage, walking up to the house. Libby, still preoccupied, came more slowly behind.

Lying in bed that night, she went over it all again, the whole incredible tableau. Went over it in disbelief. She saw the beautiful room, the attentive figures, the focus figure, the astounding things that had spilled with silver cadence from the old, dry lips.

Family, the lips had said . . . the bond . . . the obligation . . . more than these, the *compulsion*. And then she and Pierce had been subtly included as the other two in this sweet young game of mistaken love. With burning cheeks Libby recalled the little ripple of elderly applause, the sly, coy, indulgent looks.

Had it really happened? She could not believe that in this time and age an old man had actually said—no, intoned—in that beautiful voice the outrageous things he had.

But most outrageous of all had been the complete silence of the four involved figures. Perhaps Peter had not been affronted, as Pierce had suggested just now, and Tessa, Libby recalled, had undoubtedly been beyond speech. But she herself should have snapped out of her inaction . . . made a protesting movement . . . at least left the room. *Pierce* should have.

But something Pierce had said when she had flung that at him came back to Libby now; and her cheeks flamed. He had been talking tongue in cheek as he always did with her, but it did not lessen the embarrassment as she remembered him commenting of Julius Abberson's future ruling for herself and him : "I didn't disagree."

He had said it lazily, for his own amusement . . . as that mock kiss soon afterwards had been.

But, lying in the darkness, confused, uncomprehending, Libby felt a hurt, not an amusement, over the mockery, a hurt, and she had had many, such as she had never known before.

CHAPTER SIX

LIBBY'S first thoughts on awakening were the same thoughts as last night. But pondered over in bright morning light, and surely there were no brighter mornings anywhere than these Blue Mountains blue mornings, those thoughts offered a different twist. Without the recent intrigue of a chandeliered room, of an air of enthronement, of a gracious, silver-haired focus, of a sense of unreality, the episode the previous evening became just that—an episode. I imagined most of it, Libby decided, imagined that unbelievable Abberson speech. And I imagined, she told herself firmly, that gathering into Pierce Hardway's arms, or if it wasn't exactly imagination, it was certainly little less.

She showered briskly, dressed briskly, talked briskly with Barbary as she bathed and dressed her.

But for Barbary, still in spun sugar land, yesterday had been no imagination but true, and she babbled rapturously over it.

"Yes, darling," agreed Libby. "No, darling," agreed Libby. But into her new firm thoughts, as Barbary insistently re-lived the Hoon Hay fête, in her enthralment forcing Libby to re-live it as well, began to creep small doubts. Did Julius Abberson really say what I thought he did last night but had different thoughts on this morning, did he mouth words like bond, obligation . . . compulsion for those two, for Tessa and Peter? Then did he speak, ever so playfully of course, of misdirected dalliance? Insinuate Pierce? Include me?

No, it was too outrageous to be true. Libby towelled hard, and Barbary protested loudly.

"What were the bellows about?" asked Pierce Hardway, meeting them after the bath as they went down the hall to breakfast. "Is Barbary suffering from a fairy floss hangover?"

"She rubbed me too hard, Libby did," Barbary grumbled.

Pierce raised his brows at Libby, and, because he had a way of extracting answers even with his brows, Libby murmured, "I was thinking of yesterday . . . whether it was true."

"J.A.?"

"Yes."

"It was true."

"But—"

"All of it," said Pierce Hardway intentionally, "was true." There was no lift to his brows now, he looked levelly at Libby.

She wanted to ask him so much, about Julius Abberson, how he had become the spotlight that he had, she wanted to know the whole family history, but the level look disconcerted her, and by the time she had regained her composure, which was after the meal, it was too late, for Pierce Hardway was telling the boys that there was to be no slacking today, no tardy arrivals to work. "You had your holiday yesterday, and not only a paid holiday but an extra bonus in your pockets to spend."— Over the heads of the boys, briefly and remindingly Pierce sought and held Libby's gaze, reminding her that here at Clove Orange the young inmates provided their benefactor no free labour *as someone had once said*. But the look was very brief. To set the example, Pierce set off at once to the work sheds. The boys, most of them having experienced detention homes of a very different kidney, followed without a grumble.

There was little Libby could do to help Mrs. Dawson; everything in the kitchen save the mind that planned the things to be concocted there was automatic. Libby almost wished she was on the drying end of a tea-towel so that she could ask a few pertinent questions, glean some information. From past experience she knew just how much one could find out over a session at washing up.

But the plates went into the big chromium monster and cleansed themselves, so there was no opportunity to say, "I went to the Abberson Afters yesterday and heard Mr. Abberson utter some amazing things."

All the same Libby did manage to put in a few words as Mrs. Dawson assembled what she would need for a morning of cooking, to which Mrs. Dawson calmly said, "Oh, yes, it's well known what the old man plans for the two young people."

"But—"

Barbary, fascinated by the ingredients now being laid out, and refusing to move away, precluded any more questions. As little pitchers went she had *very* big ears. Besides, the ingredients also fascinated Libby. For a while she forgot the Abberson episode and watched Mrs. Dawson instead.

"Are we going to have that?" demurred Barbary dubiously, looking at a herb that Mrs. Dawson had produced. "I don't like it, it's all hairy."

"It'll taste as good as the spun sugar you were eating yesterday, Miss Barbary, and do you much more good."

"I like this one," proffered Barbary, sniffing some eau-de-cologne mint also laid out. An odd little look flicked over her small face. "I berember once we had some in our garden. But"—uncertainly—"I 'spect it's only think."

Libby edged herself round the table so that she could encircle the little girl with her arms if necessary. She knew that something was pressing itself on the child's memory . . . something gone now yet nostalgic. Perhaps Barbary's daddy standing with her in a lost garden, and a perfume from a shrub of mint enveloping them both. Perhaps this mint that Barbary now held in her small child fingers was the same to her as a pomander ball to Libby.

"I'm sorry I rubbed you hard this morning, honey," Libby apologized.

Barbary had forgotten the rubbing, but instantly took the opportunity to claim reproachfully that Libby had rubbed off all her skin.

"Would you like to have a walk in the bush?" offered Libby, contrite. "That is, if we can be spared by Mrs. Dawson." But Barbary declined. The eau de cologne mint was being chopped now, mixed with sugar, then sprinkled over big halves of golden peaches, left for the marinade to soak deliciously in.

"You go, Libby," Barbary generously dismissed.

Libby shrugged at Mrs. Dawson, who looked rather gratified if anything at Barbary's preference, and wandered out of Clove Orange.

As she went down the path, Pierce Hardway put his head out of a workshop window and warned, "I expect our new arrivals later this morning, Miss Meadows, so don't go too far."

"I won't."

She felt guilty slipping into the blue-grey bush. Even though Mrs. Dawson waved aside her help, there was still a lot she could have found to do back at Clove Orange. There was Barbary's room to turn into a small dormitory, other preparatory things. She wondered whose were the small sisters arriving of the Clove Orange parcel of boys, and if it would be Pam, her fellow cadet, or some B.W.C. housemother who would fetch them. Aware that she was not pulling her B.W.C. weight, and rather surprised because she had never been one to spare herself in the work she genuinely loved, she pushed through the bush towards the fence that separated Hoon Hay from the herbary. When she glimpsed Tessa leaning against the wire and chewing on a stem of bittersweet, she knew at once *why* she had turned her back on duty. It was because, unconsciously, she had expected Tessa to be here, and because, still unconsciously, she was determined to find out, having been included in this outrageous affair, what she felt in all fairness she had every right to know.

Tessa did not remove the bittersweet from between her white, even teeth when she greeted Libby. "I expected you, in fact I knew you couldn't stop away. I saw your face last night. You were absolutely astounded."

"You were astounded yourself," Libby pointed out.

"I was surprised," admitted Tessa. "I knew J.A., being J.A., would know all about us."

"Us?"

"Well, about Pierce and me, anyway." Tessa's tone was impatient. "But I hardly thought he'd include you and Peter like that."

"It was quite untrue, and quite abominable."

"Being abominable is Uncle Julius's custom," said Tessa, "and I don't think he's such a hot one on truth, either." She looked sidewise at Libby. "How did Pierce take the act?"

Libby said deliberately, for she was annoyed with Tessa for having put her in this distasteful position, "Mr. Hardway commented that it was almost like calling the banns. I don't think"—a pause—"he meant yours, Tessa."

Tessa bit her lip. "Pierce would be obstinate—that's Pierce. What else did he say?"

"Nothing. That's why I'm here. Tessa, I *must* know. There's more to all this than what you told me the other day, and that was the story of a patriarch's determination to hold a patriarchy together. Hold it through Peter Abberson and the girl he reared as an Abberson. You, Tessa. It was all very intriguing, but I'm afraid it was all very thin."

"It's true," Tessa said slowly. "For so long as I can remember I have been here at Hoon Hay. Peter has, too. But Peter was entitled, distantly, but still entitled. I—I had no right." The look in her face remembered times she had been told that, and Libby's heart went out to her. But she had come here to hear, not sympathize, and she steeled her heart.

"But your story of being trained to be Peter's wife, to be an Abberson wife, that's too far-fetched."

Deliberately Tessa reminded her, "Did it sound so last night?"

"No," admitted Libby, "it didn't. But . . . forgive me, Tessa . . . why *you*? You're—you're headstrong, forthright—"

"Stubborn as a mule," suggested Tessa.

"Exactly. In short surely no Abberson adjunct. So why you?"

"I suppose it's because he's spent all these years on me, and to let go now would be to admit failure, and I don't think J.A. has ever had a failure, not once in all his life." Tessa smiled thinly. "Until now. Me. For I *am* marrying Pierce."

"Well," said Libby equably, "I'm not marrying Peter. Nor anybody. I'm going back this instant to welcome three new guests to Clove Orange. And if I can get Pam, or whoever brings them up, to change places with me, I'll be leaving here today." As she said it she was aware of a vast relief. Intrigue, she decided, was not a restful thing. It diverted, perhaps, but it offered no balm. Balm! Herbs again! She smiled slightly.

But Tessa was not smiling. She was saying knowledgeably. "You won't be leaving us, Libby. You may not have an eye for Peter, and I dare you to have an eye for Pierce, but for all that you still won't be packing your bags. You're too interested now, aren't you?" Her voice challenged Libby, but Libby could find no answer, she knew it was true.

Tessa read her thoughts and smiled triumphantly. "All right, Libby, get back to your young. No doubt I'll see you around some time. Undoubtedly, too, J.A. will be seeing you."

"Seeing *me*?" Libby, who had turned to retrace her steps, turned round again. Turned sharply.

"He'd never leave things just to right themselves," stated Tessa, "not J.A. I mean he'd need to expand from last night, wouldn't he? Then don't think, my pet, that your meeting with Peter the day before the fête, the tea you took with Peter at the fête, was unobserved. I told you that tower had windows and a spyglass."

"Really, Tessa!"

"Yes, really, Libby," misconstrued Tessa maddeningly. "He never misses a thing, does J.A."

Libby had had enough. She went straight back to Clove Orange.

In front of the herbary a car was drawn up. Libby recognized it at once. Why, Daddy Perkins has come himself, she observed, rather surprised, for he was a busy man and only took on the more touchy jobs.

But she was not surprised when she went into Clove Orange. Pierce Hardway was there talking aside with Mr. Perkins, and the three new wards, lined up, were being eyed by a wary Barbary.

But instead of the three girls who had been expected, one of the arrivals was a boy, a little aboriginal boy, which would account for the presence of the B.W.C. chief, for Mr. Perkins had a tremendous sense of responsibility and liked everything to be explained.

He was explaining now to Pierce, whose welcoming smiles to the little boy indicated unmistakably that here at Clove Orange such explanations were quite redundant . . . Libby liked him for that . . . and Libby went across to listen.

She heard Mr. Perkins murmur in the soft, shorthand voice adults use to speak to each other on personal matters in the presence of children . . . "abandoned . . . charged as a neglected child at the court . . . a B.W.C. representative present . . . put it to the Child Welfare for B.W.C. to take over the boy . . . permission granted, but suggested that as he hasn't yet mixed with the ordinary school member that he finds his feet first."

Mr. Perkins went on, "In which case, Mr. Hardway, I thought, during that feet-finding, and keeping in mind that Miss Meadows is here to help . . . yes, Libby, your orders are to stay on . . . he could find them at Clove Orange. That is, if you are will—"

Anything after the beginning of "willing" was quite unnecessary. Pierce Hardway had already crossed to the little boy and swung him into his arms.

"Well, young feller," he greeted, "how do you like your eggs cooked, eh?"

If that had not been enough to welcome Edward . . . as with all B.W.C. newcomers the name was written on a tag on his pocket . . . Barbary's confidential whisper was.

"It's not eggs, it's something else. It's hairy, and it looks awful, but I think it might be nice, because most of it's here. It's called herbs. But this afternoon she's doing something else."

"She, Barbary?" prompted Libby.

"Mrs. Dawson is. She's going to sugar violets and roses, only you don't say sugar, you say Christmas."

"Crystallize," said Libby, but she saw . . . tenderly . . . that Christmas would have done as well.

For Edward had put his little dark paw in Barbary's extended one, put it trustingly, with Christmas in his eyes even though Libby had corrected "crystallize." With Elaine and Belinda . . . . it stated so on their tags . . . they ran out to the kitchen, where, no doubt, soon they would be getting into Mrs. Dawson's hair.

Excusing herself, Libby hurried after them to see they did not invade too far.

· Edward had been brought down from Northern Australia by a drover who had found him there, then, as no one came to claim him, had kept him. Originally neglected or lost, the drover did not know. "There he was," Mr. Perkins had reported, to the drover relating to the Child Welfare, "hiding behind some mulga on the

Gun Barrel track, and if he hadn't been naked as the day
he was born and knee-high to a grass-hopper, I might
have thought he was Ned Kelly, the way he was casing
me. I named him Ned Kelly after we'd got together and
I found out, through a dozen lingos, that, like Topsy, he
didn't belong nowhere, that he'd just growed. I figgered
he had to have some sort of handle."

The drover had taken Ned Kelly . . . Edward . . .
with him "on the road." He had explained, "Couldn't
leave the kid standing in the middle of nowhere." And
because, even in these days of air lift and road trains
for cattle, teams still go overland, the boy had remained
with his benefactor for a "good long spell."

"How long?" had been the question.

"From Kilcurry to Ballyup though floods held us back
at the Changeover."

When the drover had come to Sydney for a breather,
the boy had come, too. He would probably have remained with his benefactor had not a Welfare Officer
noticed the child and started inquiries.

The drover had been sorry to lose him, but he had
had to admit that he was a bit of a tie in Sydney when
you only came down once in a twelvemonth looking
forward to a bit of a bust with a big white collar to it,
so he had said goodbye to the little brown boy who
belonged to nobody, and Ned Kelly . . . Edward . . .
had been established as a neglected child.

The Welfare had found him surprisingly intelligent,
but found, too, a need for adjustment before he could
begin normal school, so when B.W.C., attending the
children's court as was their wont, had stepped in with
a request to take over Edward, sanction had been given.

Libby, watching the little boy watching Dawsie sugar
the flowers . . . "Christmas" them, Barbary persisted . . .
noted his quickness when Mrs. Dawson explained that
the thermometer standing in the syrup saucepan must
reach two hundred and forty degrees. He read and called
out much quicker than the girls.

"That's good, Edward," she praised.

"I'm Nedkelly," Edward told her . . . she was to find later that he ran names together . . . but Libby, of course, had to refuse that.

"Edward," she smiled, and touched his tag. She wondered what his real name had been, to what tribe he had belonged. No one would ever know now, for the drover, naturally enough in that vast interior, had forgotten where he had picked him up. The important thing as Libby saw it was to prepare for Edward's future and not to think about the past, so, after phoning the mountains school to arrange for the enrolment tomorrow of the little girls, Libby cornered Edward to try out his intelligence for herself. The Welfare did it scientifically, but Libby used a more down-to-earth system; she knew from past enrolments what would be expected of Edward when eventually he did attend school. She was delighted with her results. He could read a little, write a little, add up. All the old-fashioned methods, but he was sound. However, the specialists had been right when they had suggested that before he joined the other children in class he underwent adjustment.

"I want him home for a period," Libby told Pierce that night, not realizing in her absorption that she had said "home". She had explained, "He can't be expected to bridge the gap between a book told to him by campfire light and a book told in a schoolroom at one go. I feel, too, it's pretty important to let him learn about himself first, everything's so vague about him he mightn't have the least idea. So I've sent for some volumes on aboriginal lore so he can begin to discover, then perhaps come to love reading through reading not about the Swiss Family Robinson but his own people. Afterwards he can get on to the Alices and Robin Hoods the usual eight-year-olds absorb."

"Is he eight, I wonder?"

"Who knows? But we do know that drover was a jewel—why, Edward is quite advanced." Libby was silent a moment. She was seeing a camp-fire at night and a big tough man amusing himself, or, who knew? *fulfilling* himself, by teaching a small brown boy what someone once had taught him.

But Pierce Hardway was seeing her small intent face with the firelight of child love in it.

"You don't mind having a youngster around?" he asked rather gruffly. "I mean usually my customers are much more advanced in years. Small fry can be very demanding."

"I always wanted to specialize in kindergarten," she admitted a little shyly. "I always intended to enrol at a nursery school."

"Then why didn't you?"

She did not answer for several minutes. Her name had been down in New Zealand, and she had been accepted, but the course ran for a longer period than she had been able to afford—after Dad and Mother had gone. So she had had to withdraw and look for something else, something with immediate remuneration, for Paul had still been of school age. When he left school, she had intended to enrol and complete the diploma . . . only it hadn't turned out like that. When Paul, too, had gone, she had blindly turned her back on everything. On ambition. On the job she was working at. On New Zealand. She had crossed to Sydney, and, taken in all, she had been fortunate, she thought, to get a post with B.W.C. in a calling at least that attracted her.

"Why didn't you?" Pierce's eyes were a little narrowed as he repeated the question. She knew he was probing again.

"I just changed my mind," she evaded, wishing he would not keep on looking at her like that.

There was a silence between them. He still kept on looking. She knew that he knew she was not telling him the truth, she knew that he wanted the truth so that he could be kind to her as he was kind to all the boys when a hurt was there, but the soreness in her was still raw, it wanted no kindness, it wanted to be left alone to heal . . . if there was to be healing . . . by itself.

"Oh, Libby, Libby!" It was said so softly she felt she must have dreamed it, and when she raised her eyes she knew she had dreamed it, for he was looking quite impersonally at her, his lips together.

When he did open them he said briskly, "I'll be interested to learn your findings on Friend Edward. Do you intend putting him through a few tests?"

"Not exactly. I'm already aware that he's more forward in numbers than the girls." She told Pierce of the crystallized violets . . . only she said Christmas, too, and bit on her lip in annoyance. Always, she thought, I play the child in front of him. She corrected herself solemnly, then quoted a few more instances.

"I have a feeling," she went on, "that he has a sense of words. I'm going to ask him to write some little things.".

"The cat sat on the mat—or would it be better, for Edward, the frilled lizard lay by the whirly," he suggested.

"I'll show you tonight," she promised.

But Libby didn't. When she collected Edward's composition that afternoon she stood staring at it. It had taken him all day, but then he was not accustomed to a table to write on, a sharpened pencil to write with . . . probably, like the Overflow Clancy, she thought gently, until now he had written with a thumbnail dipped in tar . . . and the delight of a big sheet of white paper had urged him to go carefully, take his time. He had printed each letter. Not yet advanced to running writing, decided Libby. But it was not the neatness of the square print that compelled her attention, it was the message it told.

It said: "MISLIB LOKED AT MISTER. MISTER LOKED AT MISLIB."

She stood quite still with the page in her hand. Little

pitchers, as well as having big ears, had big eyes. *Had* she looked at Pierce in such a way that a small brown boy had chosen it for his composition? There had been so much to write about. So many things she had expected, instead of this. Not Pierce's cat on the mat, perhaps, nor his frilled lizard by the whirly, but "The hills are blue" or "I went to the creek."

But never an observation, a child's pertinent observation on two adults.

"MISLIB LOKED AT MISTER. MISTER LOKED AT MISLIB."

"Is it wrong?" asked Edward anxiously by her side.

"It's very good, darling, and it's more right than wrong. There are two s'es in Miss, and you should put Lib away from it, it's two words, you see, like Mister Pierce."

"I couldn't spell that one," proffered Edward, "so I just put Mister."

"No, it's hard, dear, though it would be polite."

"Is the rest right?"

"Looked has another O. You know O. The round one."

Edward nodded. "I'll fix it," he said.

After he had gone off with another pristine sheet of paper Libby looked down again at the composition. When was I looking at him, she wondered, and when, apart from that probing moment this morning when Edward wasn't there, anyway, was Pierce Hardway looking at me, looking in a way that a child noticed, noticed enough to write it down? When did we both "loke"?

It should have been funny, like Edward's next attempt, but somehow it wasn't, it was something that kept on turning itself over in Libby's mind.

Edward, when he returned with the sheet, had kept to the text but altered the "loke". He had made it "loooke."

"It's too many O's now, Edward."

"How," asked the little brown boy, puzzled, "do you know how to stop?"

The question stayed with Libby long after it had been asked, it stayed *and asked something of her.* "How do you know how to stop?"

Stop something you know has started . . . something you are not ready for yet.

How do you know how to stop?

After lunch Libby had a visitor. He had to be her visitor, for Mrs. Dawson, since her last illness, had been prevailed upon to spend a large part of the afternoons "lying down", but even had she been available, Libby had her suspicions that Julius Abberson would still have managed to corner her, for hadn't Tessa warned her that he would be coming, because "he would need to expand." Expand on what he had begun at Hoon Hay that night.

But, with typical gallantry, Julius Abberson spoke of everything under the sun, even the wafer-thin herb sandwiches that she had learned to make . . . "delightful, dear child, chopped chervil, you say?" . . . before he came to the point. "Spring the trap," Tessa would have sneered.

Putting down the cup, Julius Abberson smiled gently at Libby. "I fear I shocked you at the Abberson Afters," he said.

There was nothing to be gained by not admitting surprise if not exactly shock, so Libby did admit it.

"I certainly wasn't expecting to hear what I did." She took a brown wafer sandwich. "This one is rue."

"Which you felt," he suggested sorrowfully. "What a despot you must have thought me!"

Libby put the sandwich down. "I had never heard anything like it before," she said candidly. "I—" It was no use. He had said outrageous things, taken an outrageous stand, very outrageously included an innocent bystander in the picture, but Libby still found she could not say what she had said to Pierce Hardway, not to Julius Abberson's face.

Because it was such a beautiful face. Time had dealt almost too kindly with Julius Abberson's, the skin was still as firm and clear as a boy's, the eyes only a degree less bright, the hair had changed its colour but not its thickness and vigour. He was a quite lovely old man.

"Yes, my dear?" The gentle voice prompted her, encouraged her, but Libby found she couldn't protest. Not forcibly.

Weakly she complained, "I was embarrassed finding myself coupled—with Peter—in your 'misdirected dalliance'."

"Did I do such an unpardonable thing? I can't remember using such words."

"That's the trouble, Mr Abberson. You don't use the words, but the meaning still comes through."

He laughed with gentle amusement. "I'm afraid you are far too sensitive, for, apart from the principals, it wouldn't register very deeply, sadly I have to admit that none of my distant relatives whom I love to gather round me on such occasions, since, my dear, I am a lone old man, is exactly astute."

"And that's why you've designed your life to carry on with Peter and Tessa?" Libby said boldly. "Because they are astute."

"Yes," said Julius Abberson equally frankly. "They are both very intelligent, a desirable trait, I think. You would upbraid me for that?"

"I must. I mean, it's so—so—well, arranged marriages don't even happen any longer in old European royal houses."

"Not unless it is right on all sides, as it is in this instance. My dear child, my dear Miss Meadows . . . Libby, isn't it . . . I'm not being the despot you think me—"

Libby attempted a weak protest.

"I'm being right. Right. Don't you think I know these children? I've known them all their lives."

"But should that give you the right to rule their lives?"

"Not ordinarily, my dear, but this case is different."

"How different? Just because they meet your requirements? I really mean, Mr. Abberson, couldn't Peter marry any nice girl—"

"You, child?" He insinuated it so sweetly she could not feel the indignation she had cause to feel.

"There was nothing. We just encountered each other. We had tea." She was annoyed at how her words tumbled out, annoyed that she found a need to explain.

His old hand was on hers and the skin was dry but still firm. "My dear, I'm teasing you, of course."

"And you're also teasing Tessa when you say the things you do? What you anticipate? What—what you decree?"

"Decree, child?" he queried.

"It is really decreeing, isn't it?"

He smiled gravely. "Perhaps. As I told you, Tessa and Peter—"

"Were made for each other. Made by you. But, Mr. Abberson, that doesn't happen any more. Not these days. And that's what infuriates Tessa, she refuses to have her life arranged. Can't you hold her, as it seems you must hold her, by holding her in a different way?"

He was looking at her very curiously. "What do you mean," he asked slowly, "when you say 'as it seems you must hold her'?"

"I—I don't know," admitted Libby. "I—I just understand how Tessa feels, that's all, why she acts like she does."

"You mean why she throws herself at Mr. Hardway who has no interest in her at all?"

"I don't know about that, either. People often say things they don't mean, Mr. Hardway may not mean his indifference towards your ward, Mr. Abberson, I just don't know." Her voice had risen a little, but Libby was unaware of it. "I only know that Tessa feels a stricture and so she revolts."

"What a wise little person you are." The dry fingers on hers were patting gently now. "Peter would indeed have been a fortunate man had the nice girl you suggest been you."

"But you wouldn't have allowed that, would you?"

"My dear, you have just said that the days of arranged marriages are over."

"Then why do you arrange them?"

"I made an amusing little speech, or I believed it amusing, at our Afters, made it to appeal to and to entertain the only four young people present, to *include* them as it were, and from it you build this mountain." There was a little tired sigh. "Changing the subject, Miss Meadows, do you like our mountains?"

It was not just a change of subject, Libby saw, it was a close to a subject. She smiled a little ruefully and said, "I love them."

"And yet you are not Australian, Tessa tells me."

"I was born in New Zealand. Mr. Hardway believed you might have similar connections."

"Only the Scot in me."

"My grandfather used to speak of hooning the hay," Libby told him.

"Then he was indeed Scot." J.A. was rising now, carefully cupping a few crumbs that had fallen to his lap to carry them fastidiously to the window.

"It has all been very pleasant, dear child. I trust you are assured that anything I said, or, as you point out, didn't say, was entirely without malice. Give my regards to the excellent Mrs. Dawson. To the worthy Mr. Hardway. And this young gentleman is—?" For Edward had entered the room and was standing regarding him with penny-wide eyes.

"Edward," presented Libby.

Mr. Abberson reached in his pocket. He took out

something that pleased Edward much more than a coin would have, for the little boy was not up to worldly-wise money as yet. It was a colonial medal. "The Abbersons seemed to have collected such things," shrugged Julius Abberson. "That," indicating a profile, "was one of our ancestors, Miss Meadows."

Libby asked, "Our?" and at once felt rude. It sounded as though she was questioning an affected use of "Our", and she had meant no such thing. She had meant the "offshoots", as Tessa had termed them, who were all that were left of the family now, apart from J.A. himself. Was Uncle Julius including these "faraways" . . . . . . another Tessa term . . . when he said "Our"?

"*My* ancestor." There was a curiously strained look around the mouth. "I am rightly corrected. Good afternoon, dear girl. Good afternoon, sir." He bowed to both Libby and Edward.

"Can I have more paper?" begged Edward. When he got it he ran off to return later with: "THE CHEF SMILED AT ME."

"Is it right?" he asked.

"Not quite. Chief is like Pierce. It's rather difficult. There's an i before the e. That's the straight up and down one, darling."

"I'll fix it," said Edward, "but he did smile, didn't he. Is he a chief?"

"No."

"Then a king?"

"A sort of king," said Libby.

She had another visitor before Pierce came back that evening. Peter.

He came in by the side window and on the window he sat, smiling boyishly across at Libby as he said, "J.A. came down to apologize, I believe, but knowing the J.A. apologies I thought I'd better come and try to explain. Often the apology gets sidetracked."

"But can you explain?" smiled Libby.

"If by that you mean the other night and what he has set his heart on, and I think you do mean it, no, I can't, but it's fairly understandable, isn't it? He's very Family, and he loves every stone of Hoon Hay. It's only to be expected that he would have certain feelings."

Libby thought privately that with Uncle Julius it went rather further than just feelings, but decided not to say so.

"What exactly is your connection with the family, Peter?" she asked instead.

"Pretty remote, like the rest. Uncle Julius is the only pure Abberson, the others he includes are just cousins of cousins, that sort of thing."

"Tessa says the two of you became Abberson wards in early childhood."

"Yes. We can only remember Hoon Hay."

"But you at least can claim some Abberson blood?"

"Yes."

"But not Tessa?"

"No."

There was a little pause. "I wish it had been the other way round," said Peter.

"You don't want to be an Abberson?"

"No, not that, it's just that it wouldn't have made any difference to me, not like it did with Tessa. I'm genuinely fond of the old man."

"Isn't she?"

"She loathes him. As children we would fight over it, for she loathed him even then." Peter said rather queerly, "That is, I think she did."

"You *think*?" queried Libby.

"I've never really known with Tessa. Never know anything about her. Even when we played together, explored the gullies together, I never knew how she felt, how she was reacting. I didn't think much about it at all, to tell you the truth, I only thought about how I felt myself."

"How did you feel?"

"I loved her. I've always loved her. I love her now."

Peter smiled wryly at Libby. "This sudden confidence is to make me less the wishy-washy figure in Uncle Julius's little play than you must be thinking. I've never uttered an outcry, Libby, for the simple reason that as far as I'm concerned I want to marry that girl. Just as he has arranged." He got up from the window.

"Well, I'll get back now. I'm going to Sydney on the afternoon train. I only came up for the fête. I don't live here, you know, I'm a city worker. Law."

"No, I didn't know. Thank you for coming, Peter."

"Thank you for not bawling the old man out for including you as he did, for making a square out of a triangle, as it were. I saw him returning as I came down and he seems his usual confident self, not at all trampled."

"I should think it would take a very strong spirit to bawl him out, to trample him."

"Well, Tessa tries."

Libby asked thoughtfully, "Why did he include me, do you think?"

"I would say that for all his Abberson incredulity that Tessa could inveigle herself with Pierce Hardway, it was still a fairly serious thought. So he had to include you with Pierce. I can't remember his words."

"That's the trouble, one doesn't. And possibly they are never uttered, but the message is there." She looked at Peter. "How did you feel about it?"

"Flattered," smiled Peter promptly. "You're some girl."

"I didn't mean that, I meant how did you feel about Tessa—and Pierce?"

"I wish I could answer furiously that I could cut his throat, but I'm not the fighting sort ... and I like Pierce. No, I just felt sad."

Libby felt a little sad herself. He was a *very* nice young man. She waved back to him as he turned before he plunged once more into the bush.

She had forgotten all about Edward. His little dark

head was not like Barbary's bright auburn, Elaine's and Belinda's shining blonde, it merged into the background. It was still bent over the sheet of paper, so Libby said, mindful of a child's need of exercise, "Enough writing now, darling, we'll go for a walk."

It was a revelation walking with Edward. Though he did not know these mountains, he was still sharply aware of things. Things that pass others by.

"Yesterday there was a different wind," he stated. "The ferns are first this way, then that, which means the wind changed."

Then : "Something has passed here, I think a big bird."

Later : "A snake went through that grass."

Keenly : "A man with big feet was here."

"Mister?" asked Libby idly, her hand on the little crinkly head.

"You mean Mister Pierce. I can say it, but it's hard to write."

"Like chief, Edward. Can you write look now?"

"Yes. I'll show you when we get back."

But when they returned Pierce had, too, and he had taken up the writing paper.

"Is it good?" asked Edward anxiously.

"Very good, son, only you have too many e's in Peter." Pierce was not looking at Edward, he was looking at Libby.

"I don't know when to stop," Edward explained.

"Nor," said Pierce in that shorthand voice between adults, "does someone else."

"PEETER WAS HERE. HE SAID TO MISLIB ABOUT LUV," Libby read.

"The love is wrong, darling," said Libby to Edward.

She knelt down to show him, aware without looking up that Pierce Hardway was still looking at her.

CHAPTER SEVEN

TEN days had gone since Libby had come to Clove Orange. Surprising though that was, for though the time had flown she often felt she had been here all her life, more surprising still was the physical change around her in less than two weeks. It was hard to believe the difference in the landscape. Down in Sydney, and along the coast, where seasons touched hands, there would have been only infinitesimal steps into autumn, but here, in the cool Blue Mountains, almost every minute took a step towards fall.

Yet never fall, noted New Zealander Libby, for these trees, unless they were planted ones, were invariably eucalypts, and their leaves did not fall. Not that a preponderance of gums meant tree boredom, for the very word gum covered a huge and lovely canvas, and it seemed that every brushmark on that canvas was represented in this blue paradise, valleys of red, blue, silver, box, umbrella gums, the scribbly that looked like children's tracings, the spotted, the cabbage, a myriad more. Always the leaves stirred bluely and only the bark of the trunks fell off after tattering first into maypole braids of chocolate, white and cream.

But Australian autumn, foiled of crimson leaves, still found other ways of proving its approach. The nights, always clear-cut, became cameo-sharp, each star clipped out with silver scissors, the edges of the moon like a stencil. Then the mornings keened, and though end-of-summer down in Sydney merely meant a drop of a degree or two, here the temperature abruptly nose-dived and the first frosts appeared.

To small Edward from the north where all seasons were one season the change was quite bewildering if very entertaining. He came racing indoors one cool pre-breakfast, eyes like black stars. "Christmas," he gasped, "Christmas on the grass!"

For a moment Libby thought the Christmas bush that Pierce had planted had blossomed out of season, but when she saw the frost-silvered blades she said, "Oh, you mean it's like tinsel, Edward?"

"Tin-sel?"

"No, he means sugar," explained Barbary, who had run out, too. "There's sugar over everything. Just like Dawsie's Christmas violets."

"Crystallized," smiled Libby. "Of course, pets." She patted the auburn and the dark heads. "Winter is coming," she said.

"When will there be snow and jingle bells?" asked Edward knowledgeably: the drover had given him a wide education.

"That's only in countries far away," said Barbary contemptuously. "Like chestnuts by the fire."

"But there are fires here in winter," Libby promised Edward.

Edward was patently unimpressed, and Libby knew she deserved his apathy. After all, camp-fires had been a big part of his young life.

But winter hadn't. He looked out of the window beyond Clove Orange, and Libby went and stood beside him. She saw the thick bush down the valley with the forefinger of winter now upon it shown in sickled leaves, in spiked flowers with all their summer lushness gone.

She glanced to Edward to see how he was affected. Autumn was a rather sad time. But he looked more interested than unhappy. "It's like something's going to happen," he breathed.

Was it the mystique of his race or was there really something poignant out there? Libby did not know, but she felt it, too. Yet spring was usually the pregnant season, the waiting, the breathless time, she thought, not autumn.

Meeting Tessa the next day when she took Edward for a walk ... the three small girls had now become schoolgirls ... she found that she too was on edge.

"Something is going to brim over," Tessa said at once. "I feel it in me, Libby. Something's going to happen at last."

"What?"

"J.A. is going to disinherit me, perhaps," Tessa laughed acidly.

"You mean let you go?"

"I could have gone without his letting me." A proud toss of Tessa's red hair.

"But you didn't, did you?" reminded Libby. At once, at a lost look in Tessa, she was sorry, and put her hand out and touched her gently.

"We're all edgy," she confided. "Edward, too."

The on-edge feeling extended right through Clove Orange, then came to a head ... its first head ... with newcomer Elaine and her brother Bryan. Here was one instance when brother and sister did *not* need each other; Libby supposed that there was always one exception to a good idea.

They quarrelled on sight, and if it was not Pierce Hardway bawling out Bryan, it was Libby Meadows remonstrating with Elaine, though Libby had a sneaking feeling it was the brother's, not the sister's, fault. She would not say so, though; it would make her seem to be favouring her own sex. However, Pierce said it for her. One night, after he had dealt with Bryan for a new piece of victimization of his small sister, he said to Libby, "Water and oil. That pair will have to part."

"But you wanted them together."

"Not this particular set of brother and sister, this was Mr. Perkins' doing, not mine. Not all families are families. Decidedly Bryan and Elaine are not, though all blame to Bryan."

"But you couldn't—" she began.

"Separate them? I could. I might. I'm one of the

species, Libby, who do not believe that having the same blood immediately signals an affinity. I've never been absolutely happy with Bryan, and, for that matter, several others of his sort."

"But you wouldn't—" began Libby again.

"I would," Pierce said quite evenly. "Remember Paul?"

Remember Paul. Paul of the bright dark eyes, of the straying forelock of hair the same as *her* Paul.

Remember Paul!

"I sincerely hope," she said stiffly, "there will be no need to part the brother and sister."

She was aware that he was looking at her closely, probing again. "It won't tear my heart," he assured her.

But the next thing that Bryan did tore Elaine's heart. His little sister's.

"She never went to school," reported Barbary, when Libby, who had walked across to the bus stop to meet the homecoming girls asked in instant agitation : "Where is Elaine?"

Barbary added, "She couldn't go 'cos he took her bus cent as well as her piggy bank."

"Who did?"

"Bryan."

"But that would be this morning." It would have to be, Libby thought. Bryan was one of the Clove Orange planters. He had done with school. Unless he had gone up during the day he could not have taken her money unless he took it—

"I told you." Barbary was impatient. "She couldn't go to school 'cos he took her bus cent as well as her piggy bank."

"The piggy bank he took last night," put in Belinda.

"And the cent just before the bus came, so of course she couldn't go to school." Barbary added, "I thought she'd go home to you."

"I didn't," said Belinda. "I thought she'd go right

away like she said she would. Away from Bryan. She doesn't like Bryan."

"But all this happened this morning," repeated Libby helplessly. Seven hours away, she was thinking. Seven hours away is a long time with a little girl.

"Yes," agreed Belinda unhelpfully.

"Miss Tandrell says she'll have to have a note," said Barbary. "A 'scuse note."

"Seven hours," breathed Libby again.

The only thing to do, though it was distasteful to her, it made her feel inefficient even though it had not been her fault, was to go to Pierce. Libby made a strict practice of never approaching the planting or the packing unless she was asked, but this was a different situation. Not waiting to send the girls to the house, but waiting to take a hand of each in hers, for after all she had already lost one child, she fairly raced to the production corner of Clove Orange.

Barbary's brother was working on the chicory bed, and he expertly flipped a small clod of earth at his sister. The clod connected and the fight was on.

Libby forced herself between the pair, saying angrily, though she should have known that any injury suffered by either came more under the category of love bites, "Stop it, Barbary, or I'll spank you! Scott, if you tantalise her any more I'll have Mr. Hardway get rid of you, as—as he intends getting rid of Bryan and some of his associates!"

The moment she said it she knew she had spoken out of turn. It was Pierce Hardway's prerogative to break the news of an imminent dismissal, not hers. She was uneasy at the instant impact of her words. Glances were exchanged. Bryan, who was on the chicory, too, threw down his fork and said brazenly, 'So I'm getting the boot, am I? In that case I'll call it a day. How about you, Gus and Alec?"

"Oh, don't be silly," cried Libby, knowing this was not a time to argue over Bryan's, or his confederates', future. "I was just remarking that you should keep your socks pulled up, that's all, and if you want to get on the credit side instead of where you are now, you can knock off and look for your sister."

"I'll knock off all right," promised Bryan impertinently, "but I won't be doing any looking."

"Elaine's lost!" Libby exclaimed.

"You beaut!"

"She's *lost*, I tell you, and it's all your fault. You took the child's money."

Bryan clicked his tongue and said, "Fancy that."

As Libby went to remonstrate he broke in, "Look here, Miss Fields and Meadows, I never asked for that kid to be brought up here. Come to think of it"—becoming expansive—"I never asked to come up here myself. Blooming grass." He put his foot deliberately on a plant.

"Bryan!"

"Yes, Libby?"

She ignored that familiarity, there was no time to waste. "You're being extremely foolish. Where is Mr. Hardway?"

"Gone to Katoomba, or so he said, but it's my guess he's at Hoon Hay after the redhead." He laughed.

Boys were boys. Several of them grinned, and with a stone in her heart that she would never have agreed was there because of the fact that even these juniors had come to a certain pertinent conclusion, Libby called peremptorily, "Stop work, everyone, a little girl is missing."

Naturally she did not have to speak twice, not when it was an order to stop work. Tools were downed in an instant. The packing sheds emptied in a flash.

Had Pierce Hardway not had his finger on the Clove Orange pulse so continuously and so firmly that even when the finger was removed the remembered touch still counted the beat, Libby might have had a riot on her hands. But discipline was second nature now to *nearly* all these boys, and instinctively they circled her, waiting for their orders.

"Elaine Pedersen is lost. I want you to form groups and look for her, but please"—as they started to move off—"don't get lost yourselves."

"Reckon it wouldn't do any harm for some of 'em," observed Bryan Pedersen, and his friends, Gus and Alec, guffawed.

"That order to look included you three," put in Libby sharply. "Everyone will be searching."

"Ma Dawson up at the house?" queried Bryan.

"Yes." Libby whirled round, still keeping firm hold of Barbary and Belinda, and began to search the garden.

Mrs. Dawson and Edward, attracted by the buzz of activity, had come out to see what was happening. Mrs. Dawson at once tucked up her apron and made for the orchard, calling, "E-laine, E-laine, Lainey-love!"

"Mislib," said Edward, "Elaine isn't—"

"Not now, honey, it's very important that we look for her while it's still light."

"But Mislib, Elaine isn't—"

"Please, Edward, I said *not now*. Take Barbary's hand and come with me. If you see Elaine's pink dress—"

"But I won't."

"You might. You know, Edward, with forefathers like yours—"

"Four fathers?" puzzled Edward.

"You should be able to track her."

"Four fathers?"

"Oh, come on," said Libby.

"It will be no good," Edward pronounced, "because Elaine isn't—"

Libby tugged the children with her, round every barn, up the loft, down to the machine shop. "Elaine," she called, "the money is back in the piggy bank."

"Is it?" asked Barbary, surprised.

"Hush. Elaine! *Elaine!*"

"Mislib, Elaine isn't—"

"Hush, Edward!"

All Clove Orange was out searching. Libby could see the fanned-out groups examining every bush in the garden, peering behind the trees beyond the garden, a parcel of boys had gone down the valley to the creek, another parcel were scouring the caves near the small waterfall. All Clove Orange except Mr. Clove Orange himself. He was away. At Katoomba. Though Bryan had said: "It's my guess he's at Hoon Hay after the redhead."

"Elaine! Elaine!"— But he was not interested in Tessa. He had said so. He had said, "Tessa's futile breeze." But words were easy. Libby thought of how she had told Uncle Julius that people say things they do not mean. She could have added also that people can protest too much. That an abundance can often be another pointer. Oh, what was she doing thinking on these lines when a little girl was lost? Besides, what did it matter to her *where* Pierce was, Katoomba, or the Abberson mansion?

"Elaine!"

"Mislib—"

"Edward, be quiet!"

The blue Holden waggon was coming up the Clove Orange drive. It scarcely came to a halt before the driver was out. Libby and the children ran down towards Pierce Hardway, but before they were halfway there he was racing to them.

"Are you all right?" There was a staccato urgency in his voice that was almost rough. He had pushed the children from her and put both big hands on her shoulders. "Are you all right?" Now his voice was hoarse.

"Yes. Yes, of course. Only Elaine is missing."

"But you are all right?"

"I said so. Elaine—"

"Please, Mister, Elaine isn't—"

"Will you be quiet, Edward, I asked you before," snapped Libby.

As briefly and lucidly as she was able, for those strong hands still on her shoulders unsettled her, Libby explained how Elaine was lost.

He started to curse softly, remembered the children and closed his lips.

"I stopped work for the day and sent everyone looking." She waited for his approbation and was a little deflated when none came.

"Everyone?" he said sharply.

"Yes."

"Everyone—including the house staff?"

"You mean Mrs. Dawson? Yes, she's looking, too. Why, Pierce—Pierce—" For Pierce Hardway was hurrying to the house, Edward, who had dropped Barbary's hand, running by his side and intoning, "Elaine isn't—"

"Yes, son?" Deliberately Pierce paused, squatted down and put himself on a level with the little boy.

"She's not outside," said Edward. "She's inside, in her room."

So that was what Edward had tried to tell her. Libby could have wept with frustration. All this time the little girl had not been lost at all. She should have had the B.W.C. sense to kneel down, as he had, and listen to a child.

Throwing a crumb, or so it seemed to Libby, Pierce tossed, "Don't distress yourself, Miss Meadows. I mightn't have listened to him either, only I couldn't see *how* Elaine could be lost, as the last I saw of her was when I dropped her at the gate only a few hours ago with instructions to spend the afternoon in her room for even thinking of running away."

"I don't understand—" stammered Libby.

"I came out of Clove Orange just after the morning school bus left and I heard the sad story from the victim. I took Elaine with me to Katoomba"... it had been *Katoomba*, not the Abberson house ... "gave her the usual icecream solace, then returned her before I went to Hoon Hay."— Ah, *Hoon Hay* now.

"For punishment for even dreaming of leaving Clove Orange," finished Pierce, "I sent her to her room."

"You should have told me, Edward," complained Libby.

"I tried to," Edward wailed.

"But if you had said 'I saw Elaine.'"

"But I didn't, I only saw a bit of her pink dress under the bed."

"Under the bed?"

Pierce smiled, "She took her imprisonment very seriously, she's a serious little girl. Oh, well, we may as well go in, make sure that Edward is right, then call off the search."

Edward was perfectly right. Elaine was under her bed. But instead of being punished she was scared—and angry. Scared because if Bryan ever found out she had seen him from her self-imposed prison, and Gus and Alex, too, it would be awful for her. Angry because while the house was empty Barbary's and Belinda's money boxes had been emptied, too, as well as her piggy bank. And Mrs. Dawson's purse. And Libby's.

The housekeeping money. All the boys' pocket-money. There had been an attack on the office safe, but the safe had resisted it.

"And it was Bryan," sobbed Elaine, "and Gus and Alec, and if they ever find out that—"

"They won't, my pet, because they won't be coming back to ask any questions." It was Pierce. He had a very tight mouth.

He walked down the hall, and Libby ran after him.

"Why won't they be coming back?" she asked.

"Don't be an idiot!" He stopped and turned on her. "This place has a waiting list. Oh, yes, I know that must be unbelievable to you, but it has. Do you think I'd keep those wretches after all this, when other boys, decent youngsters, or at least with some potential for decency—"

"I didn't mean it that way," she interrupted humbly.

"I meant are you just going to post them as missing? Gone?"

"No, of course I'm not. I'm having them intercepted at Mount Victoria. I know the track they'll be taking, where they'll come up from the valley. You see"—reaching for the pipe but never taking his eyes off Libby—"this sort of thing has happened before. Boys have been intercepted before. It's a secret route, or so they believe —until the hand of the law descends on them when they emerge on the top. It happens, as I said. It happened to your friend Paul."

As she stood silent he said impatiently, "Now get back and soothe that baby. And next time such a crisis arises at least leave someone in the house."

"You sound," she retorted, hoping to hide the evidence of her own tears by a show of anger, "as though you expect a repeat performance."

"Look," he snapped back, "I know boys. You don't."

"I do. I do!" Paul, but *her* Paul, loved, loving. I do, she thought achingly.

"Then you should know to expect the worst. Kindly do expect it in future. And now I'll ring the police. Tell them to give the fugitives with the loot"—he looked at his watch—"another hour to climb the track up to Mount Victoria, and, they hope, the city train. By rights it should take longer, be more leisurely." He was drawing on his pipe now. "It's an extremely pretty track. There are several small waterfalls, excellent outcrops, lookdowns, leaps, a ripple of cascades. You must go one day, Miss Meadows."

"And have you waiting at the other end," she said bitterly.

"Me?"

"Or someone on your behalf, then," she cried.

"My child, when it comes to you I would never have anyone else to act on my behalf. Where, when you walked, do you think I would be?"

"Where you were today. Hoon Hay."— Oh, why had

she burst that out? It sounded, why, it sounded—almost jealous.

He was looking at her in estimation. "So you were interested in my going to Hoon Hay. I called there because—"

"You needn't explain."

"No? Then perhaps I can explain that on that mountain walk I do not pounce on you, as you anticipate, but walk with you. That we go together. And now, seeing no more explanations are needed, I shall ring the police."

Pierce was right. The boys had taken the closed-to-the-general-tourist track to Mount Victoria. Like others before them, including Paul, they had discovered the overgrown path and believed they were the only ones who knew of its existence, and its potential escape.

"Proving there is nothing new," said Pierce, after he had put down the phone from listening to how the three culprits had been apprehended and sent straight to Sydney to be dealt with there.

"But what happens to Elaine? I mean, she came as a part of a little family."

"I still intend her to be a part," he said. He flicked one of those level level looks that always disconcerted her.

Belinda had no brother at Clove Orange, and Edward, of course, was a "loner," so Elaine would not be doing anything unusual by not belonging to a family. Libby, agreeing with Pierce, murmured as much.

"But she will belong," he corrected. "They will all belong." Again that disconcerting level look. "The mother, the father, the children, the house. I believe I told you when you first came. Remember?"

As she stood silent he went on, "And tomorrow we will see about replacing our numbers, Miss Meadows. If we leave early we might even be able to bring the replacements back with us. Now, let me see what cheap labour I can do with." He pretended to consider.

"I wish," said Libby tautly, "that just for once you could forgive me for that."

"And I wish," he said back, "that just for once you could give me cause." His voice came as tautly as hers.

Across the room they looked at each other, looked a long searching time, but both finding nothing.

She is still shut in, thought Pierce Hardway. There is still no sharing for that girl, there is no outflow, no needing.

So he went, Libby was thinking, to Hoon Hay.

CHAPTER EIGHT

THEY left early for Sydney the next morning, as Pierce had planned.

Running along the deserted valley flats, Pierce had time to let his eye leave the bush road. No tortuous bends down here, no giddy heights, only the rustic curves and lazy meanderings of a track that once had been used by bullocks, and that man, later, had been either too busy or too unconcerned to change.

"As the road experts would say," smiled Pierce, "it would never have done for Julius Caesar. However, I like it. I liked it the first day I saw it, and that's why—"

"You settled on it."

"It's reasonable price as well," he added. "For rich black loam, it was a bargain. It was my luck that mountain real estate was down in the market, otherwise I could not have bought as I did, added to the first modest acreage as the herbs came good, until eventually—"

"You were Baron Clove Orange."

"Until I was a man of property," he said with pride. Justifiable pride, Libby knew, for even though, stubbornly, she would not say it, this man had sweated and toiled to win his way through. She half-closed her eyes to the blue-grey bush that Barbary had saluted so solemnly on the day of the fête, trying to picture him carving what he had out of the encroaching forest.

"A penny." He smiled at her as he negotiated a bend.

"It's not worth it."

"No?"

"I was thinking of you. Oh!" She clapped her hand over her mouth. "I'm sorry. I didn't mean—"

"That I wasn't worth even that much? Don't give it another thought, but tell me all the same."

145

"It was just an idle fill-in," she said reluctantly, still unwilling somehow to allot him praise. "I was thinking of how you must have worked."

"I did."

"Then I was thinking of Clove Orange and how beautiful it is. Really"—not withholding now—"Edward's name for you, his written name, is quite apt."

"It is?"

"Misterpiece," she smiled. "He runs names together. Quite close to masterpiece."

He smiled, too. "He's a keen youngster. Tell me what variety of child have you ordered for today?"

"Is there a new variety?" she asked flippantly. "Something besides boy or girl?"

"If there was, you'd certainly choose it just to be different. That is"—another bend—"if _I_ hadn't chosen it first. If I had, then it would be a different matter, wouldn't it? You would never choose the same as I would choose."

As she did not answer, he turned a waiting face to her.

"You've replied for me," she reminded him, and turned her own attention again to the bush.

They were climbing now, climbing up to join the Great Western Highway.

"Between the top of the Pass and the old toll house at Bowenfells it's still known as the Road of Forty Bends," said Pierce.

But now they were on the highway, and the transport trucks roared by, and there was little time for idle conversation.

At first there was the same blueness as at Clove Orange, the same fragrance of sweet earth mingled with the subtle tang of woodsmoke rising from the scattered cottages dotting the higher mountains, then civilization accepted closer settlement, and the woodsmoke ceased. Also, noted Libby, the bush lost its blueness, became olivine. Still very lovely, but for her the blue-grey.

They descended through the more populated lower mountain villages to the vast unfolding dusty gold of Emu Plains, threaded with a green ribbon that was the Nepean River, then after Penrith the run was flat as well as suburban right into Sydney.

The blue Holden waggon was parked on the area reserved for B.W.C., and Libby and Pierce climbed the society stairs.

"If you don't need me, I'll have a word with Pam," said Libby.

"I rather thought you might like a finger in the pie as well," he shrugged.

"What's the use when I'm not to be at Clove Orange long enough to be affected one way or other?" she answered, sharply conscious that she was awaiting a rejoinder—that didn't come.

"Please yourself," he shrugged, and went on to Mr. Perkins' office.

Libby found Pam, who brewed a cuppa and regaled her with B.W.C. news.

"Mary Brown has been placed, quite favourably placed. Only," related Pam, "they want her name changed to Cressida. Mary was quite impressed."

"Sounds like a name that should belong in a herbary," said Libby absently. What was being said in Daddy Perkins' office? she wondered. Were the fates of three replacements-to-be being settled? Was—her fate?

"Then those twins we had to put in Hatfield House because no one wanted twins and Daddy Perkins wouldn't have them parted are going to the country as land girls."

"Are they old enough?"

"Rising sixteen, Libby. Time marches on."

"They'll love that. They were country types, I remember."

"Cheeks like apples," nodded Pam. "How long will you be at—" She paused, then decided not to go ahead with her question. "Another cuppa?" she asked instead.

The house phone rang. It was Mr. Perkins reminding Libby to put her head round the door on her way out.

"We're evidently not stopping here long," deduced Libby. "We're evidently taking the replacements back."

She finished the tea, kissed Pam goodbye, then put her head round the Chief's door as requested.

Pierce Hardway was standing by the window, his back to Mr. Perkins. He did not turn as Libby came in.

He had been pumping the Chief of B.W.C., doing is quite openly—and unsuccessfully.

"You know as much of Libby Meadows as I know," Mr. Perkins had admitted, "probably more, having lived under the same roof for—how long is it now?"

"Over a fortnight, which is no time at all when a snail gets into its shell every time you lay on a finger."

"A gentle finger?" asked Mr. Perkins carefully.

"A touch of silk," Pierce assured him. "There is something there, and I want to know about it. When she came to B.W.C. did she confide—"

"She had the requirements we needed. That's all we asked."

"But, heavens, man, her background—"

"She was of age, we had no right to ask."

"Barely of age," grumbled Pierce. "She's little more than a child now. And a damn stubborn child. Look, I'm not asking idly. I—well—"

But Mr. Perkins had had to admit regretfully that apart from the fact that she was a good cadet ... "a real natural with children". . . . he knew nothing of Libby Meadows.

"She had satisfactory references, they satisfied the society. Anything else would have been probing."

"As well as useless," muttered Pierce. "I've probed and probed."

But now he didn't probe. He stood looking out of the window as Libby and Mr. Perkins exchanged greetings.

"We've a mixed bag for you, Libby," said Mr. Perkins. "Two boys, one girl."

"Two herb hands," said Libby in a voice for the figure at the window.

"What did you say, my dear?" asked Mr. Perkins.

"I said," said Libby, "what age?"

Now the figure turned. Turned stiffly. "*School* age," Pierce said. He did not look at Libby. "We're to pick them up from Treverton Shelter. If you're ready to come—"

"I'm ready," said Libby. "Goodbye, Mr. Perkins. You'll let me know the moment I can come back?"

"I will." Mr. Perkins went down the steps with them, something he had never done before with Libby. But then, she remembered, the herb baron, to B.W.C., was a very valuable person. When it came to accepting wards he was a rock on which to build.

The "rock" helped Libby into the waggon.

"I forgot to warn Miss Meadows about—" Mr. Perkins began to call through the window.

"Don't worry, I'll attend to that, sir," Pierce assured him. He released the brake.

As they untangled their way through the city snarl of traffic, out to Treverton, Pierce asked, "Do the replacements suit you?"

About to reply, "Would it matter if they didn't?" Libby thought twice about it, and answered, "Yes, our three girls now means we have an odd girl out, and you did say, didn't you, that we're keeping Elaine."

"Yes. Francie is a 'loner,' so should fit in well, make a good fourth."

"Is she an orphan?"

"No. Relinquished."

"Which is much worse."

"This case was even worse still, because it wasn't a matter of means, or needn't have been. However, it will be to Francie's ultimate advantage." Pierce's strong chin went out. "*I'll* see to that."

Libby noticed the singular and felt herself excluded.

"What about the boys? The rest of the replacement?" she asked.

"Twins. You know how twins are."

"Yes," said Libby, remembering the two girls who were going out to the country, so Pam had related, "twins are hard to place."

"Well, George and Harold are placed."

"What age are they?"

"Non-earning age."

"Do I still deserve that?" she muttered.

"Sorry. Ten and eleven."

"Twins?"

"Ten and eleven," he insisted. "December thirty-first and January the first. I've no doubt that George puts on no end of airs because he's a year ahead." He laughed, and Libby joined the laughter.

But she stopped laughing as Pierce guided the waggon into a side street. She knew every juvenile refuge in Sydney, and certainly down this quiet byway there was none.

"This isn't the way to Treverton," she protested.

"I wanted to have a word with you, and there won't be any opportunity after we pick up the kids."

"Yes?" she said warily.

"You heard what Mr. Perkins said?"

"Something about warning me? What did it refer to?"

"The Sellers matter," said Pierce Hardway.

"Oh—that again."

"Sorry if it disturbs you, but you have to be disturbed—and alerted."

"Alerted?"

"Sellers hot-footed it again. He's out."

"Out? You mean out of the—"

"The detention camp? Yes. Next time it will certainly have to be locked doors for that fellow. But until that happens I want you to keep your eyes open."

A little nagging worry in Libby made her retort, "Do I generally go around with them shut?"

"As regards Sellers, yes."

"Oh, that was a long time ago." It was, she thought, it was as though a page had been turned.

The car had been stopped under a tree, not a eucalyptus, but a planted English maple, so that the leaves, in honour of fall, had turned colour, instead of the bark stripping into maypole ribbons. It was a cradle of gold and crimson nursing the last of autumn in its arms. Libby thought gently of all the B.W.C. children who, unless someone opened up their heart, were nursed in no arms.

Although she was finished with Paul, the indisputable fact of his un-belonging softened her briefly to him, even though she knew now he was no good. Her mouth quivered.

Pierce was packing his pipe as usual. "You're telling me the truth?" he asked. He had seen the trembling lip. "It is finished, Libby? That maudlin attitude to that boy?"

"I said so." Her voice was stiff.

"You also said," he reminded her, "that it was a long time ago."

"It was. I think I've even forgotten him."

"Good." Pierce decided to accept that. "The important thing, of course, is that he has forgotten you."

"You mean—"

"Mr. Perkins . . . and I . . . have not overruled the possibility that he will try to see you. Hence the warning. However, if what you say is true, and I see no reason why I should disbelieve you"—he looked levelly at her— "we have no need for concern."

"And now shall we pick up our parcel?"

The "parcel" waited in the reception room at Treverton, not exactly a bare place, but utilitarian in the way such places have to be, smelling cleanly of yellow soap, floor polish, iodine applied to cuts and scratches, green vegetables and discipline.

Though not too much discipline. Matron Walters had a kind face.

"Your 'parcel,' eh?" she answered Pierce with a twinkle. "Well, here they are, all three. I'm sorry I haven't tied them up with string."

"Are they that bad?" asked Libby, eyeing the new ones at the other end of the hall, standing quietly now, as children do in times of change, the inevitable sad little cases of clothes and pitiful possessions at their feet.

"Not really. Francie is a dear little girl, and the twins are just all boy. Right you are, kiddos, be good for Miss Meadows and Mr. Hardway."

"Are they married?" asked Francie, a small girl with big green eyes.

"Mutt!" jeered one of the twins. "If they were it would be Mrs. Meadows."

"No, it wouldn't neither, it would be Mr. Meadows."

"No, it wouldn't neither."

"Quiet!" boomed Pierce. "Into the car." He added, "Back seat."

"Bags me," said the twin Harold, "not sitting near the sheila."

Pierce saw Francie's lip drop and said promptly, "Bags me having her in the front." Libby could have blessed him for that.

The twins looked at him in disbelief. "You mean you *want* her?"

"Yes."

"Do you like girls, or what?"

"Yes," said Pierce again. He stowed the thin bags, and they set off.

Libby was reminded of her last delivery to Clove Orange—Barbary, sitting beside her and saying, "I like real things, not seem."

And then the awful climax! All over the herb baron's immaculate suit.

"Penny," he said once again, over Francie's head. Francie was sitting between them.

"I was wondering," lied Libby, "where I could bed Francie. There's no space in the dormitory, I mean not until I move a few things."

"There's a small box-room that leads from your room," Pierce reminded her. "Hadn't you noticed it?"

"Of course," she remembered. "My own room is so large I haven't needed it. Come to think of it I haven't even examined it." She hadn't. She was never in her room except to sleep or dress, and any spare moment she had found she had spent standing in the closet— breathing a clove orange.

"Is it big enough?" she asked.

"Just Francie-size," he answered, and gave a special smile to the small girl.

Libby noted the kindness, and resolved on a kindness of her own for the children. She had enough in her purse.

"Last time when I brought up Barbary we stopped at Katoomba," she said.

"The real, not the seem, things," he nodded. "We'll stop at Katoomba today."

The twins in the back seat heard. They were different from Francie. They had "got around."

"Wow! Katoomba! The ice-cream cave?"

"Perhaps," said Pierce.

"I'm having," said the one Libby had identified as Harold, "strawberry special with nuts, cream, chocolate sauce, coconut and—" He must have seen a certain look in Pierce Hardway's eyes. "And a helping of spinach," he added dutifully.

Libby fished for her hanky, she had a fit of coughing.

"Cough for me," said Pierce in a suspiciously strained voice. "I have to keep my eye on the road."

The ice-cream break went off amicably, no doubt with the memory of Barbary in view Pierce keeping the twins' orders in strict check, while the twins, no doubt with their rash offer of spinach in mind, not complaining over what was in their dishes. When it was no longer in the dishes but in three contented little tummies, the Clove Orange car set off again along the Road of Forty Bends, taking the bends very prudently . . . in case . . . to home.

The homecoming, too, was amiable. The third little girl, who today happened to be Barbary, the other pair arm-in-arm and ignoring her, just, Libby knew, as she and one of them had undoubtedy ignored the third one yesterday, ran out and claimed Francie.

"You'll be my best friend," she greeted.

Francie looked shy, but Libby commended Barbary.

"That's nice of you, darling. Perhaps you'd like to keep on doing nice things, for instance help me make up Francie's bed. It's to be in the box-room that connects with my room until we can fix up a dormitory."

Barbary said promptly that she would sleep in the box-room and let Francie sleep in her bed.

"That's *very* nice of you," commended Libby again. When Elaine and Belinda came up she saw Barbary's reason. The three, at least Elaine and Belinda, were not speaking. How well Libby knew "not speaking." To-morrow, she smiled secretly, it will be someone else in the box-room.

It was a small enclosure, but snugly sufficient for a little girl. Libby and Barbary made up the bed, and by that time the bell was ringing for the evening meal.

Francie hung back, and Libby encouraged, "They're only boys, they won't eat you."

"Yes, but I don't want to eat."

"You must, darling. Everyone must eat. And I rather think you like eating. You soon emptied your dish at the ice-cream cave."

"Yes, but that wasn't grass. Someone in Treverton told me that up here you eat grass."

"Well, that would be rather funny, wouldn't it?" pointed out Libby. "It would be like sheep and goats."

"And cows and kangaroosters," nodded Francie, brightening.

Libby should have corrected the "'kangaroosters," but the brightening made her postpone it till another day.

Dinner went off well.

"It's not grass at all," said Francie.

"It's funny grub, but I like it," awarded Harold.

The games after dinner went off well, and there was not one outcry from any of the four girls when Libby declared it was time for bed. She settled Elaine, Belinda and Francie in the big room, and Barbary in the box-room. As she bent over to kiss Barbary goodnight she had an odd feeling that there were more in the room than the two of them . . . probably, she smiled, bemused, it's the hanging closets with their concealing curtains. She supposed that some of the boys' Sydney things were hung here so as to leave their own dormitories less cluttered. She would have a tidy-up tomorrow, place the clothes in order, because if a little girl was to sleep here for a few days she did not want to be entirely surrounded by shirts and trousers.

"Goodnight, pet. God bless."

A little stir. Barbary cuddling down, of course.

Libby, unconcerned, went out.

Still the amiability kept up. Libby even played a round of table tennis against Pierce. It had been, she thought, bidding him goodnight and going to her room, a very smooth day considering her companion for the day had been Pierce. Invariably something went wrong.

But today nothing had gone wrong. A word here and there, of course, but on the whole—

Libby turned the key of her door and went in.

Before she could reach the light, a hand went over her mouth. The hand still there, the bolt of the door was shot home. In the darkness Libby gasped for breath, and the fingers relaxed their grip slightly for her to breathe, then tightened warningly again.

She could see nothing definite in the unlighted room

except a dim outline. Larger than hers. As large as Pierce's.

Then she was recognizing who had her in her grasp, for the owner of the hand was dragging her to the window, pulling the shade aside so that the moonlight could show her his face.

Paul.

CHAPTER NINE

THERE was a second slackening of the hand so that again she could get her breath, but she made the mistake of framing a word with her trembling lips, and again the hand went back. A big hand...he had thickened considerably since she last had seen him, but then he was at the age when a boy grows into a man almost overnight...and a brutal one. The clasp over her mouth cut cruelly into her cheek.

He bent over to her ear and spoke softly but distinctly.

"Yes, it's me, Meadows, I've come back to the old alma mater, to the rabbits' food factory. How's rabbit food himself? Still packing grass?" He gave an ugly laugh.

She jerked her head back for air, and he permitted it. But he took hold of one of the thick curtains and warned, "No funny ideas like crying out, Libbo, or I'll stuff this down you until you can't breathe at all. I mean that." His eyes were narrowed.

After a moment he went on, "If you keep your voice down and speak into this stuff you can say a few words, but one word out of place and I'll—"

She nodded her understanding and bent her head to the floral folds of the drape and spoke into them.

"What do you want?" she asked.

"That's my girl! Right down to business." His eyes glinted approval. "You always were the pick of the bunch." As she withdrew distastefully from him the approval gave way to an ugly resentment. "Hoity-toity now, eh? I can remember a time when you weren't so choosy."

"I—" Her cheeks were flaming with indignation at his implication, but either he had no time for argument or she had raised her voice, for his hand went back, this time with the curtain clasped in the coarse fingers, which he forced, like a plug, into her mouth.

"Keep it low, you little fool, or I'll deal with you *as well as that kid behind the door*. You didn't know I knew that, did you? You didn't know I was there when you put the brat to bed. All right, I was, and one peep out of place and I'll fix the kid—and you—fast. Knowing our little Libby"—he sneered—"fixing the kid'll be more than enough. You always were a bleater."

"Paul, what do you want?" she whispered.

"That's better." He nodded. "But keep it down, as I said. I'm not visiting for fun, though"—with cool insolence, looking her up and down—"it could be for fun at that. You always were some girl."

"Paul—"

"All right, I'll tell you. I've come back to score on His Nibs . . . also to suit my own end. I need a car, in short I have to have one, and I've a fancy to make it his car. Besides"—a thin smile—"it'll be easy pickings with you to help."

"What do you mean, Paul?"

"You heard me, Meadows. You're going to help, you're going to walk out and get his keys and bring them back to me. He used to keep them hung up over the dining room door . . . a kind of goodwill gesture, I suppose, look, lads, everything on display . . ." Again the narrow smile.

"They're not there now." Libby said it too quickly for conviction, and she saw that he recognized her weak subterfuge.

"Don't try to be smart," he smiled again, but there was a warning in the hard lines of the grin. He gave a brief, significant nod towards the box-room. "Remember what's in there, Lib."

Yes, she remembered. A child was there. And while she had tucked the child in, *he* had stood and watched.

"You wouldn't—" The words were out before she could stop them.

"I would," he said coolly. "I would."

It was a bright night, but for a while the moon had been obliterated by a bank of cloud. The sliver of pale yellow sailed free now, and its thin beams lit up Paul's face. How, thought Libby, did I ever see *my* Paul in this face? How did I ever defend this boy?

But there was none of the boy now; instead a man. As tall as Pierce Hardway, almost as broad, but not set yet so presumably more agile. Alert as a panther. Watchful as a cat.

"Like what you see, Libbo?" said the hateful voice in her ear. "Sorry, honey, but there won't be time for that. I want to put miles up tonight, get going towards the border."

"Victoria? Queensland?"

"Never you mind, kiddo, just do as I say and keep your skin. Her skin"—a nod to the box-room—"as well. All right, ready to talk turkey?"

What else could she do? She stared, fascinated, at the strong young hands. Aware of her scrutiny, the fingers were deliberately clenched, unclenched.

"You see?" he whispered.

She nodded.

"Ready to listen?"

She nodded.

He inclined her farther from the direction of the door until she was almost leaning out of the window. He leaned out with her so that their voices could not possibly carry into the house.

"The key," he ordered, "that's what you have to get."

"To which car?"

"Not the big one," he said with regret. "It'd attract attention. Not the ute, it's a noisy bomb, it'd raise Cain. No, the Holden."

"If the key is there."

"It will be. Pedersen told me he still hangs it in the

old spot. Oh yes, I saw Bry Pedersen before I broke out. It's still hanging where it used to hang, Pedersen said." Sellers' lip twisted. " 'Just to show that I trust you boys.' " He mimicked Pierce thinly.

"He could see me," demurred Libby.

"That'll be your bad luck, kiddo, because if you're not back here in two seconds flat, *back by yourself,* you won't like what you'll find in there." He nodded to the box-room.

"Someone might follow me," Libby dared.

"Someone might, and it would be all up with Yours Truly." Paul paused deliberately, then said : "And with her."

The diabolical look in his evil young face set an icy finger on Libby's heart. She could not murmur, "You wouldn't . . . you couldn't . . ." this time because this boy would, and could, and both of them knew it.

"I could give a signal," she stuttered.

He shrugged. "It would still be the kid as well as me, and it doesn't take long to—"

"Oh, stop !" she gasped.

"Right, Meadows, you know what I want, but just before you go a little reminder—"

Hand across her mouth, he half carried, half impelled her into the small annexe, where Barbary slept. Together they looked down on the child, one pink palm tucked under one cheek, lashes fanned. Then, to Libby's horror, Paul took out a flick knife and held it a fraction of an inch from Barbary's little white throat.

"Hop it, Meadows." His voice was hoarse.

Libby turned and fairly ran to the door.

As she went down the passage she thought frantically : What can I do? What can I say? What can I leave as a sign? But at once she thought of Barbary, of a thin cold blade, and she knew there was no answer at all.

If only someone had been around, anyone, she still might have made an attempt, but they were all in the common-room, and by the sound issuing from beneath the closed door a final in the table tennis was being fought out. She could hear Pierce's adjudicating voice. Evidently Cahill and Phillips, Clove Orange's crack players, had reached twenty-all, for vantage points were now being pursued.

Perhaps the key wasn't there. Her heart leapt up at the thought. She could go back and tell him that, and, frustrated, he might give up and go. Scarcely had that vision occurred to her than she was racing to her room.

"It isn't—" she began hopefully, then stopped in pain. Deliberately he was twisting her arm round, holding the hand not engaged tightly over her mouth so as her agony could not find voice.

"Go back and get it. Do you think I was born yesterday? If you're not here in less time than it just took, you'll be sorry all your life." The flick knife was out again. Libby turned, and this time went straight to where the key hung, took it down and came back. He pulled her in, and closed and locked the door.

"So far so good. Does he still garage the Holden where he used to?"

"Yes."

"It's an easy getaway, the drive slopes down, I needn't start the engine." Paul added to his satisfaction a sneering, "He always was a fool."

"He trusted the boys, that's how this place functions."

"Oh, stow it, Meadows, and get cracking."

"Cr— You mean—" she stammered.

"I mean through the window with you. You didn't think"—a sneer—"I was going to be that much of a fool, did you? You didn't think I was going to leave you behind?"

"I won't raise an alarm," she promised frantically. "I won't, Paul. I won't."

"Don't be a damned idiot, because I can tell you I'm not one. I'm taking you with me. Not only will it look better if we're seen, after all a man on his own doesn't convince like a man with a girl, but the fact is I don't trust you, kid, you, or anyone. Well, what are you waiting for?"

"But what about Barbary?"

"We're not taking her."

"Is she—is she—"

"I haven't cut her throat, if that's what's biting you. Not yet."

"It'll be cold," said Libby next. "I'll have to have a coat."

"All right, grab one, then move. *Move!*"

Libby went to the closet, stood rocking a bare moment, then leaning forward, she grabbed two things—a jacket, the pomander ball. She could not have explained why, instinctively, her fingers circled the small withered orange.

The next moment he was lifting her out of the window, springing like a cat after her, taking her hand and half dragging, half flying her from the house.

The rest was simple.

"Fool," Paul Sellers kept saying contemptuously, "fool!" The ease with which he got the Holden out bore out his scorn, but then, thought Libby, Pierce Hardway had never intended bars or chains or barriers, he had had trust.

Not until they were as far as the downward slope could impel them did Paul turn the ignition key, then, tossing caution to the wind, he roared the engine and fairly leapt along the flats towards the sharp, steep rise to the Great Western Road.

It was a nightmare drive. The needle twists were difficult to manoeuvre at any time, under expert hands. In the dark, and under inexperienced hands, every bend was tortuous, every deviation of the road a hazard. At one time Libby was sickeningly conscious of a sinking sensation under their wheels, and looking down she saw that Paul had cut a bend barely an inch from a gaping gorge.

Curves raced past them like curves past a speedway

driver. Trees, bushes, telegraph posts and oncoming lights of other cars all merged.

"Paul, stop!" she gasped in sheer fear.

"Not for hours," he told her. "You'll find cigarettes in my pocket. Light me one, Meadows."

"At least put me out, Paul. I can't do any harm to you if you put me off here."

"Nor any good. I tell you I want to get as far towards the border as possible. Those cigarettes, Lib."

"I'll lean out and attract attention if you don't put me off. Paul, I'm frightened, the way you're driving you'll go over a cliff."

"Mountains finish in another few miles, we'll be on tablelands. Get those cigarettes, curse you, or I'll—"

Libby put her hand in his pocket, wondering as she did if the flick-knife would be there, and if she dared—

"No, it's not," he said above the engine's roar. "Take me for a fool?"

She found the box and brought it out.

"Light me one," he called, "put it in my mouth."

She could not have said whether what she did after that was instinctive, or whether, in truth, she could *not* light the cigarette.

At a third trembling attempt, he slackened speed, then swore angrily as he grabbed the cigarettes from her. At the same moment Libby wrenched open the door and threw herself from the moving car.

She rolled for a distance, then, struggling to her feet, she fairly flung herself down the valley that rimmed the side of the road, scratched herself on sharp bushes, at one time, in her blind panic, almost knocking herself out at the bottom of the small ravine by racing straight into a thick-trunked tree.

But at least, she thought, I'm away from him, away from Paul. Giddy, lightheaded, unreal, she pushed through the identical musks and eucalypts that were the rule of the Australian bush, through the same green bracken, the same soft ferns, the same everything, and all now, in the obscurity of night, more "same" than ever.

But it didn't matter that she didn't know where she was, where she was going, that undoubtedly she was already lost, she was still rid of Paul. That's all that mattered. To be rid of Paul.

Then she heard the staccato cut-off of an engine, and the next moment the slithering steps, the brush of undergrowth. She saw the flash of a torch.

So he *still* intended holding on to her.

Now she was badly frightened. She had seen enough of his temper before to shiver at the prospect of encountering him again. She started to run, then stopped herself. Steps would be a giveaway, she would have to play it silent and cool.

She crept forward, one foot out, the other following it. For all her breathless care she felt she was making an inordinate amount of noise.

"Meadows," he called, "come here, you damn fool! You know I'll only find you in the end and then it will be worse."

A twig tore her arm, another gashed her face. She tasted the blood as it trickled past her lips.

"Meadows, I can see you. If you don't want what I was going to use on the kid, come at once."

The words had the effect he was after. She thought, too late, as instinctively she ran...ran...ran, what a fool she had been. Now he could pinpoint her by the noise of her slithering steps, if she'd only stopped as she was—

But then, too, she remembered, there was the illuminating flash. Sooner or later, it would have searched her out. It was coming to her even now, in spite of the fact that she had put distance between her and that voice, and, violently stumbling in her hysterical haste, Libby fell over and gashed her knee. But she had the sense to remain where she fell, remain prone, and the flash passed her by.

Now it bcame a cat-and-mouse game. Libby rolled over whenever she wanted to move, she dared not rise even to her knees for fear the cat pounced.

She was so nervous she felt sure that Paul must hear the tick of her heart, as she could hear the slither and scrape of his shoes.

The moon came out, and Libby lay lower. The sharp little bushes scraped at her face, and the pungency of the bush earth stung her nostrils. What if she sneezed? Then the moon rode under clouds again and at the same time the slithering stopped, the steps stopped. But instead of relief the sudden silence brought her a fear much worse than before, it was like that nothingness you can almost touch when an engine all at once lets off steam, then is quiet.

This quiet was fraught with trepidation. Out there, Libby knew, Paul was moving towards her. She felt colder than she had ever felt before, then on top of the chill came actual physical sickness. What, she thought as she had thought of the sneeze that had stung her nose, if she was ill?

Still silence. Perhaps she was only imagining him out there, imagining, anyhow, that he knew where she was. Then there was the flash again, a wider flash than before, a flash she knew at once she could *not* avoid.

She got drunkenly to her knees, too exhausted to spring into action again, crying weakly at the pain from gash and scratch that encompassed her, at the fear of worse pain still . . . crying for just fear itself.

Then there was a shuffle she could not place. Had Paul fallen? Had he rolled down the ravine? But it sounded like more than one man.

One thing, it was certainly more than one flash, it was an army of torches. All at once the bush was lit as though it was day.

And in the night daylight Libby saw Pierce Hardway, and a police officer, and several other men . . . one of them was Peter Abberson . . . and in the middle of the

lights, struggling now in the skilled grasp of the law,
Paul.

"Libby!" Pierce was scrambling over the bushes to
her, supporting her in his big arms. "Libby, are you all
right?"

She looked at him stupidly. How did he come to be
here? Why? When? But she had never wanted to see
anyone more in all her life.

"Pierce, I—"

"Don't talk, darling, just give way, just loosen up."

"Pierce, I—"

"Here, this will help you." He pushed something into
her hand, something small and stuck with cloves and
smelling of cinnamon.

The pomander ball.

CHAPTER TEN

SHE held on to the little orange while Pierce carried her up to the roadway again, put her into Peter's car, then, after conferring with the police officers who had taken over the control of Paul, got in as well.

"I'll come back for the Holden in the morning," Pierce told Peter, who had seated himself behind the wheel, "if you'll be kind enough to drive us home—"

"Of course." Peter released the brake.

Libby wondered weakly why they couldn't return in the Clove Orange waggon. Did Pierce think it would upset her? Then, securing the door carefully as Peter eased the car forward, Pierce demonstrated his reason by turning and supporting Libby, shielding her body with his once they left the Western Road to proceed over the bumpy flats. He did it tenderly, as one would to a child, and Libby, aching in every muscle, was grateful for his gentle care.

When they reached the herbary, Pierce declined Peter's offer of help, and carried Libby to the house himself. Libby heard Peter reverse his car, and set off again down the drive.

Pierce took her straight to a divan and stretched her out. As she went to rise, he said authoritatively, "Don't move. Do you hear me?"

Libby murmured obediently, "Yes," and stopped where she was.

Her hand had moved to her pocket to encircle the little pomander ball again. Where had Pierce found it? She could remember taking it with her when she took the jacket, why, she could not have said, but how had Pierce come into possession of the small, spiked orange? Then *was* it hers? Perhaps it was another—similar—

167

ɔomander. She cupped it as she had cupped it so often, then knew : "No, it's mine."

He was back almost at once with a bowl of hot water and some towels. Testing the heat carefully, he began bathing her face and hands, his fingers infinitely careful over her injuries. Then, with a surprising feather touch for a big man, he applied a bland salve.

She said, "Thank you," in a humble voice, and again went to get up, but he said, "You've only just started, Miss Meadows. I'll do your legs next."

"But—"

He was taking off her shoes, her stockings, cleansing her bleeding feet, with a sterilized needle letting out some blisters, applying adhesive tape where it was required. Then he probed, cleansed and bound up her knees.

"Anywhere else?" He looked very big standing above her.

"No," she said in agitation, and he permitted a slight smile.

"I was going to say that if there is, then you can attend to it yourself." He placed beside the divan a small first-aid kit. "No, don't get up yet, I'll fix you something hot to drink."

Again he was back promptly, this time with warm milk laced with honey . . . and something else? . . . in a brown stein.

"Now you must tell me how you came to find me," insisted Libby, taking a comforting sip.

"I will," he promised, but there was a little glint in the promise that she did not understand—until the next morning. Then, ruefully, she knew that if he had explained, she had not heard one word. Nor did she remember him carrying her to bed. There must have been a sedative in that milk, sufficient to stave off questions until later.

And sufficient, Libby thought, lying refreshed, relaxed

yet appalled this next morning, to slip on her nightdress
before he switched off the light and closed the door.

It was Barbary who had finally awakened her. She
stood at the foot of Libby's bed and complained bitterly,
"You just sleep 'n' sleep, don't you know there's a new
child? Grown-ups is very awful, I'm never going to be
one, I think."

Considering it was always Barbary who had to be
shaken awake, Libby could have given the glowering
small girl her answer, but last night there had been the
possibility that Barbary wouldn't become the grown-up
she despised, and Libby, thinking of a thin flick-knife,
gave a shiver.

"Are you sick or something?" said Barbary, contrite.

"Something, darling, and I'm sorry I wasn't awake.
I'll shower at once and see to the new child."

"He did," explained Barbary.

"Pierce?"

"Yes, and he's been in here a hundred million times.
Here he comes again, with tea. So you are sick."

"No, just—" Inspiration came to Libby. She knew how
Barbary loved to manage. "I don't suppose," she
appealed, "that you could take over the new child?"

Barbary, full of importance, fled before Libby could
change her mind.

Pierce put the tray beside Libby, then sat on the bed.
She watched him as he poured two cups . . . so he was
staying for a while . . . then handed her one.

"Want to be propped up?" he asked.

"I think"—embarrassed, and she hadn't wanted to be,
or at least to betray it—"you've done enough."

"My dear girl," he shrugged, "you couldn't go to bed
in all those clothes." The shrug helped, and so did the
casual tone. Libby felt herself relax.

"You put something in the milk," she noted rather
mildly.

"It was strictly herbal."

"But why?"

"You had been under a considerable ordeal, your nerves were in rags."

"Then you're not blaming me for not raising an alarm? I thought of it . . . I even tried . . . but you see. Barbary—" That reminded her of the thin, evil flick-knife. With Paul's remarkable adroitness he still could—

"The police found the knife at once," said Pierce. "I gathered that that was what he used on you, through the child. But it's all over now, and no skin lost, except your skin, Libby. How are the wounds this morning?"

"I feel fine . . . then after a bath—"

"One is running right now. Sorry I can't stop to replenish the bandages after it, but I must go up to Hoon. Hay. But before I do"—had he noticed a quick stiff set to her jaw that Libby could not fail to feel herself, and had he determined to avoid any queries as to why he must go up to the house on the hill? to Tessa? by repeating quickly, "But before I do, I'll tell you what happened last night."

"You noticed the key gone?"

"No, I didn't, or at least I wouldn't have had I not had need to use it. I trust the boys. Clove Orange is run on trust. But I needed to see the Abbersons."

"Again." The interruption was out before she could prevent it, and he gave her a quick, sharp look.

"I needed the key," he said stolidly, almost expressionlessly, "so I went to get it, and it wasn't there."

"Hadn't you heard the car?"

"Not at the moment. There was a rowdy game on and it would have been difficult to listen to oneself think. But something must have penetrated, unwittingly, for as soon as I saw the empty ring, I knew, in retrospect, who had happened."

"But how would you know that?"

"The idea had occurred to me," he said, "that Sellers might try this. I will admit that I never anticipated he would try it through you. Even though you've never

answered me when I have questioned you about h
I still believed the matter had closed."

"It had."

He only hunched his shoulders at that.

"Then—-then why did you include me in it?" she
asked a little helplessly. "Anticipate that I had gone, too?"

"I ·didn't rush out as soon as I saw the key was
missing," he replied. "Naturally I checked the house
first. When I saw that your room was empty, I had a
shrewd idea of what had taken place. It was smart of
you," he awarded, "to remove the clove orange to tell
me for sure."

"I did it instinctively, I can't remember thinking
about it."

"And probably you laid it down instinctively, too,
when you leapt out of the car. Can you remember
placing it on that prominent road post?"

"Why, no. Did I?"

"I blessed you. It marked you there as surely as if
you'd left a twelve-foot sign. I caught sight of it as we
prowled along the Western Road, for naturally we knew
that Sellers wouldn't hotfoot it back to Sydney but hit
west. Even though the car wasn't there, but round the
next bend, I had Peter pull up. The police pulled up
after him."

"How did Peter join in?"

"I'd gone there first," he said. He added levelly, "But
this time for help."—This time?--"It only made sense
that we took Peter's much more manoeuvrable car in
preference to my big one, to the old ute. Well, that's it.
I think you can fill in the gaps yourself."

"But why" ... the words were unspoken on her lips
... "are you going up there again now? It's always
again. And again." As though she really uttered them
she clapped her hand over her mouth in dismay.

"Libby." He spoke as levelly as he had before, but
his eyes held hers. They *asked*.

But she couldn't answer. She couldn't answer for two

sons. One was the same reason that had kept her lips
ut before, an embarrassment that he should learn her
nterest in him. The other was the reason that words
had flown from her, flown in a sudden discovery that
left her dumb in disbelief. She couldn't . . . She didn't . . .

But Libby knew she did.

She loved this man. She knew it by the almost suffo-
cating largeness in her heart. Now she understood why
she had shrunk from telling him about Paul, her own
Paul, about her parents; it was because his sympathy
would flow over her, his gentleness, his tenderness, and
tenderness, because she was bereft, was *not* what her
heart demanded.

She knew now she had always loved him; even standing leaning over a banister and calling down impertinences she had loved him. She had not recognized those
impertinences for what they were, pitiful defences
against being found out. Found out loving a man who
did not love you.

For it was quite clear now who Pierce did love. He
had protested, yes, but that had only been his lips protesting, not his heart. Like the eternal male, he had
clung jealously to his single identity, even made a con-
vincing show of his protestations. But all that was over
now. Tessa had won. These frequent visits to Hoon Hay
were done with the hope of wearing Uncle Julius down,
for after all, even though Pierce, on his own words, was
comfortably placed, the money that must come to Tessa,
even though, unlike Peter, she was not of Abberson
blood, should not be dismissed without trying first.

"I hope it comes off," she said sharply. "I—I hope
you—you get the loot as well as the girl."

He looked at her stupidly for a while, then slowly he
followed her trend. He leaned over the bed, and for a
moment Libby believed he was going to shake her, or
strike her, and she half-flinched.

That brought him to his feet. Away from the bed.

"You have very long claws, Miss Meadows," he said.

CHAPTER ELEVEN

AUTOMATICALLY Libby got up, bathed, attended her injuries, then went out to the "new child."

Francie had settled in well, even to the extend of already having squabbled with her "mother," and consequently three-d off with Elaine and Belinda.

That left Barbary and Edward together, and Edward was being Barbary's baby, which did not offend him so much as amaze him, for possibly, and probably, the little boy had never known a mum. Certainly not Barbary's variety, anyway. Barbary issued shrill orders, alternatively kissed and spanked. The spanks were only tokens, and set Edward laughing, but the kisses he ducked away from whenever he could.

"They're wet," he told Libby.

"Kisses have to be wet," declared Barbary. "I berember once—"

She stood still a little while as she often did, groping back for something, and Libby's heart went out to her. When would she start to forget? It would be better for her to forget.

She went to the kitchen to Mrs. Dawson.

Mrs. Dawson looked cross, there was no doubt about that. Had last night's upset put her out? Had Pierce left the first-aid bowls unemptied? things about? Perhaps she was sickening for another migraine attack.

"No," said Mrs. Dawson, reading Libby's look, "it's him. Up there again, at Hoon Hay. Seems to me"—reaching for the rue—"he should take residence up there."

"Peter is there, too," offered Libby.

"I know. I've been wondering if it means anything, if they're coming to a family agreement. Of course she,

173

essa Abberson, would like to do away with formality. Her idea would be to run off with Pierce and then toss her marriage lines triumphantly at old Mr. A., but whatever Pierce is, he's a stickler for doing the right thing."

"Then why are you complaining?" asked Libby a little tautly.

"Because it's the wrong thing, for Pierce. Tessa's wrong. *I know*." Mrs. Dawson put in more rue than necessary, so added another herb to detract from it. "It'll be a queer dish today," she shrugged.

Everyone seemed out of sorts. When Libby put her head round the packing shed she saw that all was not well on the production line either. The boy whom Pierce had put in control had a minor mutiny on his hands.

"What is it, Robert?" she asked.

"They won't do as I say, and Mr. Hardway told me—"

"Mr. Hardway didn't tell you to ask us that way," complained one of the mutineers.

"I wish he'd get back," fretted Robert.

Everyone wished it. At dinner Mrs. Dawson's dish plainly was not liked, and, without Pierce to jolly up the occasion, encourage the boys to eat it, if only (by surreptitious winks) so as not to offend Mrs. D. and so render rosemary cream, a universal favourite, a definite non-starter for future meals, it was a sober gathering. Barbary pinching Elaine and Elaine throwing her potato to Belinda and Belinda settling it all by pouring her milk over Francie, except that Edward got most of it, made it no better.

We need him, thought Libby. Then, tremulously, hopelessly, her heart changed that to *I* need him. But what was the use? He was up there. At Hoon Hay. With Tessa.

The meal came to a desultory end. The boys went back to work. The four little girls came together again in a busy game of Houses, which cut Edward out, for he had never known a house before this one, he had only known sky and stars for a roof, or, if it rained, a rough canvas shelter.

"He doesn't understand anything about a house," dismissed Barbary loftily, ruling all around her from the role of mother into which she had inveigled herself once more. "I'm sorry, Edward, but you can't play. Elaine, sweep that floor while I make a pie. Francie and Belinda, make the beds."

Edward thought it was rather silly, so did not mind being cut out. Libby suggested that he wrote things while she did some mending. There was always mending to be done.

"MISTERPIECE," wrote Edward, "IS GONE." He sucked his pencil a while, then wrote: "MISLIB IS SOHING."

"S-e-w, darling, it's one of those hard words."

"SHE," wrote Edward, "IS SADD."

"Only one D., Edward." But Libby did not say she was not sad.

She supposed as she snipped the grey thread from the patch in James Wilson's shorts that it would have been little use protesting. These Australian sons possessed that extra sense, or so people said.

Then she became aware that Edward was no longer writing in the absorbed way that he did, tongue out and curling with the curl of the letters, little puffs and grunts.

"Edward," she said gently.

No answer.

"Edward."

The little dark boy came slowly back to her.

"Lost," he said.

"What is lost?"

"It isn't a what, it's a one. A people one. And I don't know which one is lost."

"Oh, Edward, don't be foolish, we're all here, safe and sound. Only Mr. Pierce isn't here, and he—Edward, what do you mean? Who is lost?" There was an awful humping in her heart. Pierce couldn't be, and yet this aboriginal child—

Edward said again, "I don't know which one."

She pumped him, but he had lost the thread and had returned to his writing.

"MISLIB IS NOT SEWING SHE IS LOKING AT THE TREES."

"Two o's," said Libby.

Now it was she and not Edward who was being psychic. Something *had* happened, she could feel it in the air. There was a sort of waiting, a sort of suspension. A chill fingers touching her.

Five minutes later Pierce Hardway ran up the path.

Libby was out of the room in a flash, running down the hall to meet him.

But he pushed past her, going straight through to the kitchen and taking up the big bell that was kept on the shelf. At one time, Libby remembered, following in spite of the rebuff, he had told her that it was only used in extreme emergencies. When it was rung it was rung hard enough to re-echo to the packing, printing and processing sheds, farther out to the planting. It rang one message only. "Drop everything. Come here."

"Pierce . . ." She had to break through to him even though the grim expression on his face did not encourage interruption. "Pierce, are you all right?"

"Yes. It's trouble, though. Hoon Hay. I'll tell you as I roster the boys."

"Hoon Hay?" she echoed bitterly, and this time she did break through.

Turning on her, the bell giving its last clang, he said, "What do you mean by that?"

"I mean the name of the house on the hill. You should know, you're there often enough."

The boys were surging back to Clove Orange, coming with much more alacrity than they had gone, the tenson had broken, the waiting had finished, the suspension that evidently they, too, had felt was about to be dissolved.

He was looking at her narrowly, trying to gauge her words. But when he spoke it was quite impersonally.

"That is so. I had something I wanted to do up there."

"Presumably." She spoke flatly. "And Peter, too, was needed, apparently."

"He was." Still impersonal.

As she did not follow up, he said, "I think you know what I was about."

"I think I do. Is—is it settled?"

"It might have been, but a disaster has intervened, and I mean disaster. To be lost at any time in this mountain bush is grave, but when it's an old man—"

"Lost?" Edward, Libby thought, Edward sitting with his paper and pencil but not writing about Misterpiece, murmuring, "Lost—" instead.

"J.A.," said Pierce.

"But he knows his own environs. Mr. Abberson must know."

"Not as much as you would think. He lived in his ivory tower, not in the green world around it. Besides, he has been ill, that's why I've tried to force things before—" Pierce paused, then explained, "You see, the doctor had issued a prognosis nil . . . no hope . . . and I wanted to—"

He had wanted to settle the question of Tessa—and himself. And why not? Why not? Yet Libby's heart cried secretly, "But why?"

Pierce did not explain any more. The rest Libby heard with the boys.

"Mr. Abberson of Hoon Hay on the hill is missing. He has been ill, his mind disturbed, and during the disturbed period he has evidently wandered out, no one knows where, and now grave fears are held for his safety.

"All work will be suspended while Clove Orange joins the searchers. We will go about the searching in a calm, methodical manner, for only harm, even a second disaster, can come from a haphazard, if enthusiastic, hunt.

"All seniors now will report to me, pick their squads, decide their method of operation. They will agree to scour the valley, the foothills, the mountains or the gorges. Once they decide they will do only that territory, but do it thoroughly, leave not one bush unexamined, no creek bed discarded, no overhang of rock.

"All right, Jones, Smithers, Ferguson, Quilter to begin with. Over here." Pierce glanced briefly at Libby. "You can keep the children out of the seekers' hair, help Mrs. Dawson. Everyone knows that an army of searchers is only as good as the food to fuel them."

It was dismissal, and Libby, dismissed, went out.

Mrs. Dawson was already busy on preparations.

"Yes," she sighed at a question, "I've done this sort of thing before. The mountains are places where people regularly get lost—weekend walkers, young explorers, adventurous people leaving the tracks to see a different aspect and thinking it will be a simple matter to find their way back. Only it's not. It's a deceiving bush. Pierce says it's enigmatical. Is that right?" Mrs. Dawson started buttering a toppling pile of bread.

Libby, who had gone to the window to stare out, thought grimly that Pierce's was the only description. A strange, enigmatical country, fraught with the stilly hush and the breathless mystery of the unknown, of the eternal question of the new and the young as well as the sere and old. A fascinating but frightening country, achingly beautiful in its strange blue air, but still secret and withdrawn.

"And," Mrs. Dawson resumed, "when it's an elderly person it's much more worrying, for a night out in these mountains can, and has been, fatal. Especially when the lost one is in bad health."

"If Uncle Julius is in a weak state he may not go far," Libby pointed out.

"Near or far, it's still as hazardous. You've seen yourself how hard it is to pinpoint anything in our bush."

"What is the usual procedure, Mrs. Dawson?" asked Libby.

"There's a regular mountains rescue squad up here. They will have volunteered already, then the Flora and Fauna Society will lend their help, the Bush Walkers, every local man, unless he is disabled, will turn up, all the police and brigades. If it goes on overnight, the army will send up a squad, possibly a helicopter. But even then—" Mrs. Dawson sighed.

"He could collapse anywhere," she resumed. "In a bank of bracken. Behind a rock. Short of scouring every inch, and that would be impossible for all that Pierce has ordered it, there's a grave danger of not getting there in time."

"You mean the night and its drop in temperature?"

"I mean before that, too. Pools, deep ones, that the stumbling feet of a sick man could fall into. Then there's the usual snake and spider hazard ... once in the rain forest, where, in a fever, he might reach, he could be bled dry by leeches. But my guess is that exposure will do the damage. He's old now, and frail."

"And quite beautiful," Libby said abstractedly. She could see Uncle Julius moving down a graceful curve of steps through a smiling guard of honour, his silver hair shining like a halo, his thin, delicate, perfect hands touching young heads, his sweet, gentle smile.

"Yes," agreed Mrs. Dawson practically, "but frail." She began filling the bread slices.

"Can I help?"

"Of course. The children can, too. We'll have more than our usual army to feed today. You could start them on the potatoes, if you think you can trust them with a scraper. You know Pierce always says that potatoes are as important as a pair of binoculars, or a police dog. They can't find, but they can fuel someone who will."

"I'll get them," said Libby.

The four girls were still playing houses, unaware of the act now being played.

"Look," scolded Barbary to Francie, "I want this floor washed so I can eat from it."

"Haven't we any plates?" asked Belinda.

"Of course, but I berember my mother used to say that."

For a moment when she had come into the room and not seen Edward, Libby's heart had faltered. Surely the little boy had not tagged up with one of the searching groups? She could imagine Pierce's biting criticism if Edward, too, was found missing. "You couldn't even watch a child," he would say.

But Edward was not missing, he was writing again.

"THE PEOPLE LOOOKED AND LOOOKED BUT ALL THE TIME HE WAS NOT OUT THERE."

"Too many O's Edward. Come with me now, darling, we're all going to peel potatoes."

"For chips?" asked Barbary.

"Perhaps."

"I'm not peeling for boiled, I don't like boiled."

"I don't like smashed."

"Mashed. Now come along."

She set them on the floor with a big dish and five innocuous scrapers, and they scraped happily enough, scrapped just as happily, and occasionally became less serious over their job and began to potato-carve instead.

"Mine's a bear," said Francie.

"It looks like a fat boy."

"Like Edward."

"He isn't fat."

"Well, he's a boy."

Libby smiled tolerantly. What if they had grown tired of being useful, they were still only babes.

Then Elaine said, "Where's Edward?" and Libby did not smile. She noticed with a hollowness that this time Edward *had* gone.

"Where is he?" she echoed Elaine, advancing on the girls.

"He just went," informed Barbary airily, "he didn't say where. I noticed when I was his mother he was a nawful child."

"He'll be back at his writing." Libby spoke her relief aloud.

"I don't think so," advised Belinda, "he went out of the house."

"Why didn't you tell me?" wailed Libby.

"Did we have to?" Four small faces lifted innocent eyes to Libby.

"No, you didn't, darlings, it was my fault. Just keep on making things with the potatoes."

"You said to peel them for chips."

"Not for boiled or smashed."

"It's mashed," said Elaine, "Libby said so."

"And Libby says DON'T GO OUTSIDE THIS ROOM." Libby stood over them to make sure they understood the message. When they looked sufficiently impressed, she hurried out to see if by any chance Edward had returned to his chronicle of Misterpiece and Mislib.

He had not. She had not really expected he had, it had been just a faint hope.

She did not feel so concerned for Edward, for intrinsically she sensed that the little boy could more than cope with a position like this, but she did feel concerned for herself; Pierce, she knew, would spare no words.

She had taken up Edward's last piece of writing.

"THE PEOPLE LOOOKED AND LOOOKED BUT ALL THE TIME HE WAS NOT OUT THERE."

Had Edward been writing for writing's sake, or was there a message here? He possessed that extra sense, like all his race, she was quite convinced of that. Had he not felt their present disaster before any of them even had known that Uncle Julius was lost?

"THE PEOPLE LOOOKED AND LOOOKED BUT ALL THE TIME HE WAS NOT OUT THERE."

Not out where?

Not where the people looked? Where they were still looking?

That was down the valley, up the mountain, in the gorges, on the creek flats. In short, the bush.

So, interpreted Libby, Uncle Julius was *not* in the bush.

He could not be in the house, as Elaine, posted lost, had been, for the family would have exhausted that possibility at once. But he could be in the vast grounds of Hoon Hay, and that made sense, for in his delicate condition he might not have been able to get far, even though a fever will often lend strength to weak limbs and carry a sick man more miles than a sound person.

It was all ridiculous, for the grounds, too, would have been searched, and except that Edward had written what he had, dark-eyed, dreamy Edward, Libby would have dismissed her own thoughts.

But instead she ran back to the kitchen to see if the girls were still occupied ... and they were .. then, with a word to Mrs. Dawson, she ran up the short cut.

Even as she pushed through the wire she thought how absurd she was being, already a squad of searchers would have hunted the ground until not a stray leaf remained unexamined.

The pink walls of the mountain castle merging into the blue tiles that merged into the blue sky and into the blue bush held her a moment on the Hoon Hay side of the slope, then pushing upward she began a systematic search. She passed the formal shubbery, the avenue of wisteria, the planted cold weather trees, the acre of velvet grass where the fête had been held.

No, it was quite absurd, Edward had simply been writing words.

All the same she did the other side of the house, an

empty house, no doubt, even the help that J.A. employed were also out searching. An errant idea occurred to her. Was Tessa out searching? Brittle, rebellious Tessa, longing to shake off her Abberson fetters but bound by something she did not understand yet could not hold off, Tessa, who hated J.A. but who, when his dry lips touched her brow, had averted her own eyes so he could not see the tears.

But Libby had seen them, and wondered . . . *just as she wondered now why Tessa was huddled in that remote corner of the Hoon Hay grounds, under a large oak, a concealing oak with—why, it was Edward.*

She went quickly, silently forward and sank down beside them. Then she opened her eyes wide. Tessa looked up at her but did not speak.

Edward did.

He said simply, "They were looking in the wrong place, so I came here. I liked him, he gave me a medal. When he saw me he told me to get her." He nodded to Tessa.

The two girls gazed at Uncle Julius, who lay prone between them in a grassy hollow beneath the tree. It was easy to see how the searchers had missed him. But on the other hand it was quite impossible for both of them to believe that Julius Abberson had directed any such thing to Edward, for the old man lay quite wraith-like, even death-like, seeming beyond all aid, decided beyond issuing directions.

Edward must have sensed their disbelief, for he insisted, "He did."

And at that moment the papery eyelids opened, focussed and found Tessa, the old lips spoke. At first the words were not clear, then, bending nearer, Libby heard them, saw Tessa's drained face as she, too, heard them, for they were spoken to her.

"My child. My own child," Uncle Julius said.

"My daughter."

CHAPTER TWELVE

THERE was no more work that day, for many of the squads had gone quite a distance, and it had taken considerable time to call the search off. Pierce did it by strategic fires that would convey a message with the knowledgeable rescuers by Very light. With the closer seekers he simply stood on an outcrop and cupped his hands and called "Found!"

Back to Clove Orange they all came, in singles, in twos and threes, in squads. Mrs. Dawson's sandwiches were welcomed, and, washed down by the hot sweet tea that Pierce had prescribed for fatigue, the boys and men soon recovered, and after standing around discussing the search shook hands and left.

"It's not always," said Pierce, watching them go, "such a good ending."

"Good?" Libby asked in wonder, for there had been no doubt in her mind that Julius Abberson was slipping away very fast. Then she looked at it from Pierce's point of view, for it was Pierce who had carried the old man into the house, had stopped with him until the doctor's arrival. And, thought Libby, no doubt he had found at last that opportunity he had been seeking all this week to tell J.A. while he was still conscious that Tessa and he—that they—

"Yes, good." Pierce interrupted her thoughts. "He has always been a formal man, it would have been saddening for him to have perished instead of"—he paused—"dying. Yes, Libby, there's not long."

"I knew it when I saw him," she nodded. "I just couldn't believe anyone so frail could have walked even that far. How did he do it? Why?"

"It's remarkable how even the frailest person can cover

a distance if the spirit is strong. And J.A.'s spirit was strong, it had a purpose. He wanted Tessa."

Libby nodded. "Edward told me he asked for her."

"Yes, Edward," considered Pierce a moment. "It's your turn to tell. How did that child know where to go?"

"Someone else would have to tell you that, it's something I can't understand—but something I recognize."

"You mean you believe the race possesses an extra sense?"

"I'm sure of it," Libby said.

"But the wonder is how you read Edward's intention, for you did, didn't you, you went up to Hoon Hay and searched in the grounds yourself."

"Edward had written," Libby related, "'THE PEOPLE LOOOKED AND LOOOKED BUT ALL THE TIME HE WAS NOT OUT THERE.'"

"And you found a message in that! You, too, are psychic."

"No, I just happen to have been with Edward more than anyone else." Libby added, "You have explained how but not why J.A. tottered out to where I subsequently found him."

Pierce said, "He would have been quite exhausted, and of all the places he could have collapsed it had to be a remote corner like that, a concealed corner, for I'm sure the ground searchers would have scoured very thoroughly."

Libby persisted, "But why? Why did he go? A fevered brain?"

"No, I would say it would be quite clear. He went, of course, for Tessa. Tessa had not been near him . . . not an unusual attitude with her . . . for days. But I had been near him—"

"For days," Libby said levelly.

"That's right. I had been trying, appealing, reasoning, driving, even coercing to endeavour to break through. I knew he had not long to go, and I didn't want him to leave like that."

"Like—like not recognizing you and Tessa?" Libby asked.

"Me and— Oh, don't be a fool. I've told you how I've always felt about that before."

"Yes. Told me," she said flatly.

He was looking at her, looking sharply. All at once he snatched up her hand. "This is going to take longer than I thought—and hope. We'll walk down to the outcrop and say it all there."

"I have things to do. I—I'm leaving, of course."

He said, "Of course you're not."

"I—"

It was no use. His grasp was iron. Short of pandemonium which one did not display in front of the young there was nothing else but to obey that iron grasp.

Libby walked with him down the path, through the bush, to the big rock.

"We'll start from the beginning," he said, "and try to keep it in words of one syllable, for you're not acting very bright."

"Perhaps that's what I am. Not very bright." Her bottom lip was thrust out.

He said unexpectedly, "But you are. You're a star."

She looked at him quickly, uncertain of what he meant, or even if he had meant what it sounded.

But he was not ready for that yet, he indicated with a shrug of his shoulders.

"From the beginning," he insisted, "and that, of course, is J.A. You know now, and I think you guessed all along, that—"

"I didn't guess. How could I? How could anyone?"

"But you saw in Julius Abberson someone you had seen before," Pierce reminded her.

"Yes. But I never thought—"

"Well," intervened Pierce Hardway, "I did."

"But how could you?" repeated Libby. "How could you see that Tessa was—"

"Julius's daughter? The likeness fairly jumped out a me."

"But his age. Then Tessa's."

"Seventy-odd. Twenty-odd. It's not such a gap. There are many autumn children, though in this instance I will admit that Tessa was more a winter child."

"And he never—he never—" Libby could not say it, it was too cruel, she thought.

"Never recognized her." Pierce did say it, said it firmly, impersonally, determined not to judge.

"Why?" asked Libby again.

"That's harder to answer, and yet, knowing Julius Abberson, not hard at all. He came from a very strong-willed stock, an autocratic stock. Look"—indicated Pierce of Hoon Hay, looming majestically above them—"that edifice is J.A. himself. No mere mountain house for an Abberson, but a castle, a palace, a tower."

"Was his denial of Tessa because she was female?" put in Libby shrewdly. "I know that some men—"

"Undoubtedly," agreed Pierce, "it would be an affront to a strong personality like Julius Abberson's to receive a daughter and not a son. But no, that is not the answer."

"Then—?"

"Julius Abberson married very late in life, he brought to the marriage all the Abberson glory, perfection, the record of success, never failure. And then—"

"Yes?"

"The marriage failed," Pierce said.

There was silence a while, then Pierce looked down the valley and narrowed his eyes in thought.

"Can you imagine the shock of failure to someone who had never known it, whose family had never known it, had only known the importance of continued success? Can you imagine the resentment, the hate it bred?"

"Against Tessa?"

"In the beginning, yes, but then the curiosity, the urge, the compulsion of one's own flesh and blood break-it, had only known the importance of continued success?

s far"—Pierce now took out his pipe—"as accepting
Tessa as his ward."

"It's all so incredible. Surely some of those aunts and
uncles and what-have-yous must have known."

"Not necessarily. The line of Abberson, the *pure* line,
was a single line. Those relations were very distant—as
J.A., being J.A., would want. Also, I doubt if anyone
would have known that Julius Abberson had married. He
was over in Scotland at the time. And he was never a
communicative man."

"How," breathed Libby, "do *you* know all this?"

"It's been with me, if uncertainly, for years . . . ever
since I came here. Tessa and Peter were only school age
then, but to me it fairly shrieked out who was the
Abberson. And it was not Peter."

"Then why was Peter included in the Abberson plan?
That is, if Tessa is right in what she told me and there
was a design and plan."

"To assure the name of Abberson continuing through
their marriage? Yes, there was. But I can't tell you about
Peter. Perhaps he was one of those distant relatives, as
he has been told. Though perhaps J.A., having given
in to his urge to have his daughter with him, cast a
deliberate eye round for another child, a suitable child,
a likely one. And, of course, *a male*."

"So it was Peter."

"Yes."

"Poor Peter!"

"No, not poor Peter, poor Tessa, because she has the
Abberson blood. And yet"—for a moment Pierce stopped
smoking—"there are qualities in the blood. It's just that
obsession for perfection, for nothing short of perfection.
Of absolute success."

"It must have been a blow," said Libby quietly, "when
the biggest thing of all in life, marriage, didn't succeed."

"I agree. Mrs. Abberson had left Julius before the
birth, walked right out of his life. No doubt she had
cause, but I don't think J.A. made much of a success in

his choice of partners either, for she immediately aban-
oned the child.

"J.A. didn't tell me how he discovered Tessa, though
it would have been easy enough, for that sort of woman
would undoubtedly have written for money. All I know
is that eventually he took Tessa in as his ward, at the
same time he took Peter as a ward, *but an Abberson one.*
And there, Libby, is Abberson rearing its ugly head. To
punish Tessa for having the mother she did, she was
branded non-Abberson, and Peter claimed instead."

"It's all too fantastic," she said softly.

"It is, and yet it's true. The preparation for marriage
that J.A. practised between Tessa and Peter was also
fantastic, but it's also true. He trained those youngsters
to take over Hoon Hay, in the name of Abberson, after
he'd gone. Only one thing went wrong—Tessa. She was
a true Abberson and she would not be told what to do.
She revolted against what she could see was being designed for her, no matter that it might be what she
wanted herself, and she tried to escape, but for all her
forthrightness there was Abberson blood in her, and
though she didn't understand she still felt an affinity to
the place, and to J.A., as strongly as anyone has ever
felt, I think.

"A few weeks ago Peter told me his uncle was failing.
Peter is a fine man. One hundred per cent."

"How did Peter take his non-belonging—if it is that?"

"The good thing is it doesn't matter either way, not
with Peter. If he is not even an offshoot, a faraway, as
Tessa puts it, he will remain unconcerned, he's one of
those uncluttered people who simply love for love's sake.
He loves old J.A."

"So," said Libby, "does Tessa."

"Yes—but what an Abberson love that is." Pierce shook
his head. "But, like her father," he continued, "there are
qualities, and I have to admit them, but, by heaven, I'm
glad it's Peter, not I, who will have to find them out."

"Peter? But— You mean—"

"Those kids loved each other right from the beginning. Really loved. If ony J.A. hadn't stressed his point they would have come together anyway. Why, you couldn't have kept them apart. But the Abberson fire in young Tessa revolted, and because she was an Abberson she had to fight. So she set on me, only"—he tapped his pipe—"it didn't work."

"You didn't—love her?"

"Good heavens, she's a fury, she's a whirlwind, never my type. Besides—"

"Yes?" breathed Libby.

"I had already made my own Abberson plans, and by that I mean plans made in the Abberson manner, definite, not to be waved aside. I had decided, on sight, on my girl and what was to be."

"You're very clever," said Libby.

"Very," he answered confidently, "considering she took an instant dislike to me, so instant and so viperish that only I had decided, Abberson-decided, my design, I might have changed my ideas."

"You didn't?"

"I never have, Libby, never from the first time you leaned over a balustrade and shouted out to me."

She stared at him, disbelieving, suspecting the words he had said, not crediting, not even remotely accepting . . .

"I tried to reach you," said Pierce. "I tried every way I knew. Sometimes I felt like tossing it all in. If I can't reach this girl, I thought, what's the use? And it's still the same now. You always withdraw. Why, Libby, *why*?"

She was still looking at him stupidly, still not believing, still not crediting . . . .

In a voice she hardly recognized as her own she said, "It was all so recent, I mean I couldn't bear to touch my own pain, let alone let anyone else."

"A brother? A brother rather like Paul Sellers, was that the reason you were a fool over that boy?"

"Yes ... but several months before Mother—and Dad."

The tears were streaming now, she tasted the salt of them with surprise, knowing that this was really the first time she had cried.

"And you locked all that up in you," he said tenderly. "Why, oh, why?"

"It was sore," was all Libby could offer.

"Of course it's sore. And will be sore. But it will be like your wounds the other night, growing less painful because of a balm, a salve, a gentle touch.

"Libby, let me be the gentle touch. I need you, darling. Apart from a memory of two fine people who took in an unwanted child I have nobody—except a parcel of boys."

"Four girls." Her voice quivered.

"You have it behind you," he went on, "the birthright, the family, Libby. I want it before me, want it desperately. Help me, my love."

As she still looked at him in disbelief, he said quietly, "I know I've rushed you ...I know you can't possibly feel this way yet, but Libby, this time don't get back in that shell so quickly, just—just give me a chance."

She felt for the pain, the old familiar pain to hide in, the pain of parents, of brother, but all at once the pain was not there. A sadness, yes, a nostalgia, but a resignation as well. It had happened, and she could not alter it, and—and—

She shut her eyes a long moment. "Pierce," she whispered, "be my gentle touch."

They sat on the outcrop until the blue bush began to fan out indigo shadows.

Looking up to the house on the hill, to Hoon Hay, Libby said, "Why, it must be nearly night. They're pulling down the flag."

"I think," said Pierce softly, "it's for J.A."

Back at Clove Orange Mrs. Dawson was making rosemary cream. "I felt the boys deserved it," she said.

"This boy?" asked Pierce with meaning.

She looked at him, looked in hope, found her answer and said, "Now this time it will be right, not wrong."

The girls were playing school. Edward was writing. "MISTERPIECE AND MISLIB WENT OUT."

"We're back now, Edward," said Pierce, "and we've something to tell you. Very soon instead of Mislib you must write Mrs. Pierce."

"MISUSPIECE," wrote Edward. He stopped curling his tongue to ask, "What does that mean?"

"That we're married. Or going to be."

"What's married?" Edward asked next.

Libby kissed the crinkled top of his little black head.

"It's sunlight on stone walls," she told him. "It's mown hay. It's flowers." She smiled at the herb baron, *her* herb baron. "It's a pomander ball."